Turning Baseball
UPSIDE DOWN

Turning Baseball
UPSIDE DOWN

Memoirs, Truths & Myths
From Coaching Baseball 55 Years

ALEX GAYNES

Enjoy!

Library of Congress Control Number: 2020900423
ISBN: Hardcover   978-1-7960-8154-1
                 Softcover   978-1-7960-8153-4
                 eBook   978-1-7960-8152-7

Print information available on the last page.

Rev. date: 01/13/2020

To order additional copies of this book, contact:
Xlibris
1-888-795-4274
www.Xlibris.com
Orders@Xlibris.com
807787

Contents

Foreword

Alex Gaynes is not your typical baseball coach. A lawyer by trade, he coaches baseball every summer despite the searing temperatures of Tucson which eclipse 100 degrees almost every day. He is unique as he shows up for games with open toed sandals and a massive 52-ounce mug of Diet Coke.

In this day and age of coaches calling virtually all pitches on the high school and college levels, Alex simply refuses to do it.

He wants the catcher and pitcher to work together and instructs both on how they can exploit weaknesses of hitters during games when they come into the dugout.

His teams are allowed to play the game of baseball by making mistakes early in the season. If a runner tries to take an extra base and is thrown out, Alex will not give that player a dirty look or scold him. Instead, he will pat him on the back and tell him what great hustle he showed. This strategy allows his players to take the extra base without fear and serves them well in tournaments.

I have been editor of *Collegiate Baseball* newspaper for many years and had the pleasure of interviewing the top head coaches in high school and college baseball over the years, including Hall of Famers such as Rod Dedeaux of USC, Skip Bertman of LSU, Mike Martin of Florida St. and Augie Garrido of Texas, just to name a few.

The common denominator with these elite coaches was that they constantly got the most out of their players. Alex Gaynes has done the same, and this book explains how he did it for so many years with a system that can't be beat.

He also has been a servant/coach for all these years, and his players love this man. Many tell him that playing for his teams were the best days of their lives. Enjoy this book and relish the concepts he teaches.

Lou Pavlovich, Jr., Editor/Publisher
Collegiate Baseball Newspaper.

Prologue

This is a story about life and baseball, or maybe about baseball and life by a confessed baseball coaching lifer whose every attempt to retire has failed.

So I decided to write about it. After all, it's like my wife tells me, just tell stories. So that's what I have done.

The problem is, that every time we talk, we are reminded that there is another story to tell. At lunch today with sons Josh and Carl (who both played for me, though not always willingly) we were reminded of the Legion season that Josh caught a full season of double headers unbeknownst to us with a cracked bone in his ankle.

While eating I received a text from son, Rusty (who like Josh, also coached with me) coaches an MSBL team in Phoenix. He is having a terrible season, and has entertained thoughts of retiring. I sent him a draft of this manuscript today, and received this text while eating lunch:

"I've been ready to quit coaching after this season. After reading chapter 1, I am not ever quitting!"

Thanks, Rusty. I hope you like this.

Introduction

"Coaching Sandals barred in eight states and mug."

I am a baseball dinosaur and something of a Maverick. My philosophy is quite different than most, as you will soon see.

The National Office of American Legion baseball has enforced a couple Alex Gaynes rules because I came to the West Regional tournament one year with ONLY 10 players (we had 9 for our State tournament, which we won, so we thought we were loaded). Because of me they changed the rule to require a team to have at least 12 players. Why? I'll never know.

When I was scolded about having only 10 players, I asked the organizers whether they had changed the baseball rules, since you only need 9 to play. They said no, and basically threatened us to do well. I told them if we didn't do well, we wouldn't come to any more regionals. I think we've been to 9 since.

I didn't understand their griping. I guess, I'm just one of those old time guys who would rather have nine or ten guys who actually play, than have a loaded bench of PO's (pitchers only). Of course, this means that you have to play your players, and my goodness, they may need to play multiple positions.

One year our catcher was drafted and signed away from us. I needed a catcher, so my two ace pitchers, Kyle and Joey agreed to alternate between pitching and catching. That's the way it worked on our Legion teams.

We never had dissension on our teams. Everybody was too busy playing!

My sandals were banished from our local American Legion Baseball league a number of years ago. Luckily I'm still allowed to keep score in the third base coaching box, though many people don't really like it, (which is, I guess, one of the reasons I do it).

Somehow I've been allowed to coach-for 55 years now-and have not been drummed out of the core...yet.

In all those years, I did not made a dime (far from it) from coaching (though I did receive the princely total sum of $1,300 (total) recently for helping coach the JV baseball team at a local high school 25 miles from my office- 3 hours per day, 6 days per week for months on end.

I've never gone out and recruited "the best" players from our Tucson community, never promised a player that he would become a major leaguer or college player if he played on one of my teams (though I have had a part in coaching at least 12 guys who made it to the major leagues, literally thousands of others who didn't and hundreds who have played college baseball), and never lost my amateur status by charging people to take advantage of my coaching prowess. Caveat to parents: if someone tells you that you need to spend a lot of money to play or your kid won't make it to the majors, run from them as quickly as possible.

My former players coach at every level of baseball, including at least 33 who are currently coaching in little leagues and for club teams in Tucson (goes to show you I must not have turned them off from baseball too badly), many are current college players, many are minor league players, three in the majors, and a whole host of them are great citizens.

I've coached at every level: T-ball, Coach Pitch, Minors Little League, Majors Little League, Pony Baseball, Junior, Senior and Big League Little League, Legion, Connie Mack and even helped start a local Collegiate League-the Sun Belt College League. My KFC sponsored Legion team was one of the most well known teams in America.

To give a better perspective into my odd ball ways and coaching philosophy, I include a letter from an imaginary friend which I used before giving the key note address at the American Legion West Regional Banquet in Phoenix a couple of years ago, to kick off the West Regional Tournament.

I had been charged with obtaining a speaker for the tournament. I arranged for Jack Howell, a 7 year major leaguer with the Angels, an MVP in the Japanese League, the field director for the Seattle Mariners (now with the Angels), and former Hitting Coach of the Arizona Diamondbacks. He played Legion ball in Tucson, played for our local JC, and then moved on to the University of Arizona.

At 3:00 AM on the morning of the speech he called me. He had a family illness and would be unable to attend the banquet and give his speech. Here I was, without a speaker. And on the day of the big event!

When I called the directors in Phoenix, they told me we did have a speaker. Guess who was elected!! When I opined that I didn't have a clue as to what to say, my wife chimed in: "You're so full of it, just go out there and tell stories. People love it when you do!" That's what I did, and that's what I have done in this manuscript (along with some baseball and life advice sprinkled in here as well).

That's what I decided to do, kicking that speech and this book off with a letter from an imaginary friend. Hopefully this will help you decide whether or not to read my other meanderings.

My imaginary friend wrote:

Dear Alex:

I heard that you, of all people, will be giving a talk at the American Legion West Regional Tournament Banquet.

Whatever possessed those people to invite you when they had JR Howell.

I mean, you are some old guy who never gives a sign, stands at the third base coaching box with your score book, looking like a "schlump" (that's a Jewish word meaning "schlump"), keeping score. You drink no water and always carry around a 52 ounce Circle K mug filled with Diet Coke.

That's just not done, Dude.

Your teams come out in dirty uniforms that look like they haven't been washed in 6 months (and probably have not).

Your teams run bases like wild men. You must think that you'll get a medal for having guys thrown out.

Of all the stupid things, I saw you send a runner from second on a fielders choice ground ball to second in a 0-0 State Championship ball game. How the heck he was safe, I'll never know. You were so lucky to win that state championship.

Of all the stupid things you did! You had that little second baseman on your team for years, and every time he got to first he stole second on the first pitch. What kind of stupid baseball is that. It's only because the kid was fast that he was safe all the time.

Your guys never seemed to get to games until just before they started. And the players you picked up. One guy ran a red light which resulted in a fatal accident, another had an affair with one of his teachers, and still another streaked the Catalina Foothills HS graduation ceremony. What were you thinking, where are those dead beats now! (Answer, a well regarded lawyer with four kids, a professor at a major Catholic university, and the third one is a PHD candidate in physics at the University of Arizona)

Why in heavens name would you go to tournaments with only nine or ten players (including Regionals) I'll never know. [Hint to my friend]: Because everyone gets to play.

That you would win 10 Arizona State Legion Championships, 2 Connie Mack State championships, 14 Southern Arizona Connie Mack championships, 2 Pony Championships and three Little League championships is a travesty. You couldn't coach your way out of the Lincoln Tunnel.

By the way, can my son play for you next summer?

Yes, the letter is true in many respects. Yes, I coach third base and keep score. Yes, we go to monster tournaments with only 9 or 10 players. Yes, we steal second base on the first pitch all the time (stop us if you can!). Yes we take a scoring lead from second every time we are on second. And yes, believe it or not, over the years we have won most of our games.

We particularly enjoyed, over the years, beating those club teams with multiple sets of uniforms and over filled rosters.

I remember once we were playing in the High Desert Classic Baseball Tournament, a 50-65 team event. We were playing an amazingly talented Colorado team sponsored by a Denver area car dealership. They had 18 players, more than one set of uniforms, and numerous players who had college scholarships, many of whom had been drafted.

Of course, we had little chance of winning. Well, win we did. Quite handily.

After the game their Coach came up to me and insulted me, our coaching style, our players, our uniforms and anything else he could throw at me.

My response was simple.

"You may have 9 D-1 players, the best Colorado could offer, many drafted players and really spiffy uniforms, and a huge travel budget, but it is you who should be ashamed.

"My catcher did not catch one high school inning. My third baseman was thrown off his high school team, my shortstop never played short before (with good reason, JJ Hardy late of Oriole fame was ahead of him on the depth chart), my first baseman has a broken ankle, and my third baseman had to put the shoulder joint of my catcher into place after a particularly dirty collision at home.

"Yet, if we played you ten times, we'd beat you nine of them. It is you who should be ashamed."

That night another Colorado Coach (with whom I never got along until then) called me at our hotel and thanked us for beating those guys.

So, what is it that I have to offer? What pearls of wisdom do I have to offer?

Read on.

Chapter 1

Just What Is It That We Offer? The Golden Rule

What is it that we offer? Just this.

Rule 1: Coaching is a sacred trust, and goes way beyond coaching. You owe the players your best effort. You owe them the duty to care for them.

Rule 1A: Let your kids play. They are not robots and need to really learn how to play. You don't have to be as drastic as I was (steal on first pitch, always go first to third on a single to right, always take a scoring lead from second, if you think its going to drop, then run like a wild man. If its caught, the coach is an idiot, if it isn't caught; great running)

Rule 1B: Understand that your influence as a coach extends far beyond the white lines.

Rule 1C: Have passion for what you do, because it rubs off on the kids, and it's over before you know it. Darned, I can't believe I'm 72!

But above all, love your kids.

One of the best compliments I ever received was not meant as a compliment and told me how great a coach the man who said it was, and is. We were in the midst of the Arizona State Legion Championships. As almost always, Post 7 and their Tucson Hall of fame coach Oscar Romero and my KFC team were locked in a fierce struggle for the State championship. I was probably acting like a total butt and was railing at everybody running the tournament. People were yelling and screaming at me in very negative terms. No swear words of course! Right!

At one point Oscar Romero yelled at me from the stands, and I'll never forget this because it told me why he is such a great coach, and why I'm pretty damned good myself:

"Come on Alex, we love our kids just as much as you love yours."

There it is, the key to the whole thing. Passion and love for the kids and love and respect for the game.

When my son Rusty played for me he told me that he knew yelling at him was a sign of love, but could I please love him a little less.

For years people have asked why kids seem to play better for KFC than their ability. That's it folks, all in Oscar's phrase.

Love the kids, love the game and live it with passion.

I will close this chapter with two stories that always cause me to be overcome with emotion. Just before the day of the speech I received a text which illustrates my point.

1.) Christian Muscarello — Text from his Dad, Mike Muscarello

"Hi, Alex. I just wanted to thank you again for not only coaching and accepting and giving Christian the opportunity to play for KFC, but for all 3 of my sons. I know Catalina foothills players have been irresponsible and didn't have the courtesy to honor their commitment to you, so I'm extremely grateful for your belief in my boys.

Michael-Shea still talks about the most fun he ever had at any level of baseball [helped a bit by back to back to back home runs with his brother in the State Championship Game] was playing for you and KFC. Your dedication, passion and love of the game is extraordinary! You should be recognized for everything you've done for so many players for so many years! Again, thank you for everything you've ever done for all 3 of my boys. Most importantly, thank you for being a big part of Christian's life!"

That week Christian signed with the Cardinals.

2.) Braxton

The final story I told (please understand dear reader, that I see life as a series of vignettes) is about a kid named Braxton.

He only played 7 games at third base for me, and that was because we were short players in a 52 team tournament in Albuquerque, so his coach loaned him to us. Obviously they weren't going to loan me a star. And, he was not a great player, but he played his heart out. He regarded it as almost a sin for a ground ball to get by the third base side of the infield. When the tournament was over, our players were lying on the field, totally spent. He threw me his jersey. I threw it back to him telling him he earned it. You would have thought I gave him a million dollars. He didn't take that smelly darn jersey off. Not at dinner, not that evening, and not on the ride home.

A few months later Braxton died in a one car accident on his way home from Junior college. His grandmother sent me a card thanking me for all I had done for Braxton from just one tournament, one darn tournament. She also told me he was buried with his most favorite possession, his KFC jersey.

That says everything.

Enjoy it, love it and live it, Thank you..

Now on with the show. But one word of caution. The opinions rendered herein are mine, and solely mine, and not that of the management.

Chapter 2

The Big Lie: Money Is
The Key To Success

The Big Lie: Unless you pay me thousands of dollars and play for my Club/Travel/Elite/Select/Show Case/All Star Super Team, your kid will never make it to the major leagues.

The Truth: This insidious lie is propagated by those who want to soak you blind. Recruiting the richer parents to go with their "selected" players is not a formula to create a major leaguer. It doesn't even mean the kid will be a good player, ever. What it does mean, is that you will help fund the new Mercedes for the Coach.

Sorry guys, because a guy claims to be an ex-major leaguer does not mean he is one, or that he can coach a lick, or that your player will benefit from it. Check the Baseball Encyclopedia to find out if he really played in the majors-every player appearing in a game is listed.

Yes, their teams will win a lot of games. They should win, they recruited all the best players in your area!! But that doesn't mean a fig about being a good coach or the right fit for your child. Or that it is good for your child. Baseball is going the way of AAU basketball. Kids would rather hit a long fly to the warning track than move a runner and perhaps win a game.

Don't get me wrong, there is no sin in paying someone to give your son batting or pitching lessons. But the truth is, most of them charge a lot and aren't any good. Many guys will sell you a bill of goods, however.

My son, Rusty, spent years hitting most Saturday mornings with Jerry Stitt, the hitting coach for the University of Arizona.

4

I regarded it as money well spent. Why? Jerry was a terrific coach, and was also a truly nice man whose philosophy and insights were as meaningful to me as was his hitting instruction.

Our son, Josh, was a favorite catcher for Brent Strom, the recently acclaimed pitching coach for the Astros. Brent was a no- nonsense guy who coached many in the Tucson area. He charged reasonable fees, and was a terrific teacher. He loved Josh who he often said was his "go to catcher." Josh was one of those kids who simply gave it all, whether it was catching for a Brent Strom lesson, or was playing a game. Brent recognized this and even got Josh a job as a bull pen catcher for the Tucson Triple A Pacific Coast League team.

Be sensible and protect your player's arm.

Brent was one of the good ones. But, just because Brent gave you lessons does not mean you will become a major leaguer, or even a college player. Parental expectations, often result when parents have spent a great deal of money on their player, and forget about the physical well being of their player.

Chapter 3

The More You Spend, The More You Endanger Your Player

Tommy John surgery has become an epidemic.

The worst part of these travel/club team adventures is the damage that is being done to pitchers' arms. They often do not practice, and show up on weekends at costly venues to play in tournaments. Nothing in youth baseball is more disastrous and destructive to young pitching arms than Club/Travel teams.

I'm sorry, I don't want my kid (or yours) not throwing during the week, and then being expected to throw in a tournament.

Mechanics are truly important. Some of the teaching methods do more harm than good. Have you ever wondered why a softball pitcher can throw and throw and throw, yet a baseball pitcher can not? I ascribe a great deal of that to arm circle. Try this. Take a baseball and put it in your hand. Then lift the ball straight up to your shoulder.

Where do you feel it? In the shoulder. Now take the ball and pretend you are getting ready to lead a symphony orchestra. Use a conductor's motion to lift the ball up. Where do you feel it? Nowhere, unless you are doing it wrong and my instruction isn't making any sense. If you use a proper arm circle, your arm will have more life. But even the best arm circle in the world can't protect against abuse and overuse.

Believe it or not, as old as I am, I often throw 600-900 hundred pitches per week during practice. Yet my arm is rarely too sore to do it again the next day.

There are a couple of local coaches that use the phrase "from the thigh to the sky" to describe a proper pitching motion. If your son does that, make sure to keep a nice reserve for surgical intervention. Start your young player right by teaching a nice, safe, smooth, arm circle. That does not mean your player won't ever have a sore arm, but it decreases the chances.

It was very frustrating when two of our high school pitchers this past couple of years had Tommy John surgery before they could drive.

Don't buy the hogwash that your player will get "better exposure" and "be seen." If he's good he'll be seen. Protect his arm. Save your money.

The new way to throw your money away is on so-called "showcases." Who benefits from these expensive events? Certainly not the players. Who gets the attention at a show case? The 6'4" pitcher who throws in the 90's. Do you think this kid needs an expensive show case in order to show off his 90 plus fastball? And what about the kid who runs to first in seconds flat. Does he need the show case?

Who needs the showcase? The 5'8" second baseman who is a terrific player day in and day out, but who is overlooked at showcases, even though they need the showcase the most. They are neglected. Size, and the ability to hit the home run are looked at as more important than fundamentals. If not big, or powerful, his natural attributes won't be startling enough to engender the excitement of the "scouts." Sorry, he won't be drafted.

My exposure to "Club" baseball has both been good and bad. One year I was asked with my friend Steve to coach an 11 year old team at a local hitting facility. We did so, and it was a terrific experience.

We didn't purposely just recruit great players, we encouraged kids who just wanted to play ball, and coached the dickens out of them. We ended with 30 players on our two teams. Here is an amazing fact: Every single one of those kids ended up playing varsity baseball in the Tucson area. Not one of them had Tommy John!

Another time, we decided to experiment by taking guys who either were not selected for, or did not get to play on the local Amphi Little League Senior League All-stars. We made a deal with our kids. If you come to practice every day, we will work as hard as we can to get you better, and we promise you that by the end of the summer and the beginning of the fall, you will be better than the so-called All Star team.

We fielded that team more than 20 years ago. And work we did. And improve they did. By the end of the Fall, our players were far better than the supposed all star team. Virtually every player made a varsity high school team, and a number went on to play JC and 4 year college ball. One even became a head college coach. We were proud of these guys. We proved a point, and are still proud.

In fact, one day while coaching our JV squad one of the parents called me aside and asked if I knew a certain individual and asked if his son played on that team. It turns out that he did. He said the father (who helped us coach) to this day talks about our team, and what we did for those kids.

Yes, a coach has an amazing affect, both good and bad on players.

Chapter 4

Play And Trust Your Players

I have found over the years that players do not get better unless they get to play. Believe me, trust them. They will step up and improve. The Little League bench sitters rarely get better, and soon lose interest and leave the game.

A couple of seasons ago, I was coaching the JV players at a local high school. We started out the season with 30 players and two teams, JV A, and JV B.

By mid season we were down to 13 players. For various reasons, including grades, and some misbehavior, we no longer had our three best catchers (and believe me, Junior Varsity teams rarely go more than one deep at that position), our best shortstops, and, perhaps even worse, we lost a couple of our better pitchers.

We were now forced to play guys who barely received a look during tryouts and early season games. We just knew that the rest of our season would be a disaster. No way we could compete!

How wrong we were!! We lost a couple early, including perhaps the best game we played all year by one run to a really good program. We then won 9 of our last 10, including our last game against, by far, the best JV squad in all of Tucson. As they won games, they began to feel better about themselves. They avenged a couple of early losses, and beat a team for whom I coached for one day before getting fired (which is another story).

How proud we were of those kids.

We pretended to be unconcerned as our best players were stripped from us, and told the kids we didn't care "who wasn't there." "We cared for the ones who were there." We had no idea they would step up like they did. But, in truth, we should have. I had seen it many times throughout my coaching life. I guess it wasn't often enough to really believe in what I knew to be true.

How silly was I?

Nine years earlier, I was coaching a grandchild in Little League Majors. As usual, we were quite successful, in a conference with teams from a number of other Little Leagues. Though we finished in first place, we were placed at an extreme disadvantage by having to play the top three teams, and expend our pitching resources, in the 9 team league, just to advance to the final round.

Our least talented player was a boy the kids called the Sausage. I'm not sure why, but it was a term of endearment, not ridicule. Throughout the season he asked me daily if he could get to pitch. I told him if he worked really hard, perhaps we'd make it so. He was at the field early every day, pitching to his dad.

Well, we got to the championship game of our league tournament, but because of a 14 inning game (one of the greatest Little League games ever played) that took three days to play, we had no pitchers left to put on the mound. So, against the wishes of our other coaches ("what, are you crazy!"), we pitched the Sausage, with specific instructions. He was to walk their two good hitters (the lead off and number 4) and pitch to everyone else.

He did everything we asked for, and shut out a team that had a walk to the championship and had their ace fresh and ready to go. You should have seen the pride in his parents' eyes. We won the championship and the kids selected him as our most valuable player.

As we left the field I was confronted by a mom from the other team.

"You're nothing!" She said.

"If it weren't for your coaches, you'd be nowhere."

"Thank you," I told her. "I guess I'm not as dumb as I look!!" Give kids a chance, and they'll play for you.

A few years later I was working in my office late and received a call from my friend Steve (one of our coaches). "Alex, you have to come and see this!" "The Sausage is pitching for Santa Rita HS against State Champion Desert Christian." I was so excited, I dropped what I was doing and left my office midstream. I just had to see this. Here was a boy who would never have continued in baseball had we not believed in him enough to give him his chance.

"The Pride 2018, unlikely tournament winners."

It is really a sad commentary these days. So many kids leave the game because they are not really given the same chance that other kids get. They sit on the bench, and play the least amount coaches are allowed. Give the kids a chance. You'll see, I guarantee it.

We decided to challenge the current vogue that only club teams that recruit the best players play real baseball, by giving an unattached group of kids a chance to play.

So in the fall of 2018 we started a team from a local religious private middle school that did not have a year round baseball program. The last time we had done the same thing, the team turned into a back to back to back state champion at Desert Christian high school. The associated High School was nicknamed the Lions, so we called ourselves the "Pride."

The school allowed us to announce the start up during morning school announcements. Our mission: to start a program that would welcome players from the school, regardless of ability level. Our goal: to begin a program where the kids could play together prior to high school. We were not interested in "launch angle," money or assembling the best players possible. We simply wanted to give some kids a chance.

We started with our hands tied behind our backs, since most of the more talented 7th graders were already playing on local area club teams. We were going to be playing on a large field with a group that, if they had played at all, were just graduating from the small Little League field and played in a league not known for developing players. Compounding the problem, most of the kids either were on the school cross-country team or were playing middle school football.

We practiced every day (the soccer and football teams did not) so that every player could practice with us on days cross country or football were not playing or had time off. Since almost every day kids were missing from practice either because of school, school cross country or football (and even soccer for some), teaching our players was a challenging task.

We also had two boys who had never ever played a game of baseball in their lives. Of our 11 rostered players, these two had the best attendance records. Neither player was particularly athletic or physically mature in any way, yet, both kids hung in there day after day.

Believe me, it took patience to attempt to bring them to the level of kids who had played ball most of their lives. Luckily Brian and Josh, who were terrific coaches, were up to the task.

It is a big jump from Little League with 60 foot bases to a field with 80 foot bases.

Patience became the most important ingredient for coaching this team. We worked on fundamentals every single day, starting with the most basic ingredients. Rolling balls to infielders, right left catch, right left throw. Throwing balls to outfielders (at the start it was too dangerous to hit flies balls to some of the players).

Hitting off tees, and playing our one strike game and line game, everyday. The line game and the one strike game will be explained at length later in this manuscript.

Progress was slow. We started our season losing our first game by 10 runs, and repeating the performance during most games.

I kept telling my wife and the kids that they were getting better all the time. No one gave up hope and continued to work hard.

But after each game I was chided by my dear wife and others: "Do you really think they are getting better?" Yes, I really thought so, though I am sure my wife doubted my sanity. But I could see it, I really could. Honestly.

During one game I had one of our new kids lead off (boy did I take guff for that). Somehow he reached base each time he was up.

No, he didn't hit the ball hard, but he got on base. His base running was a real adventure. We were playing real baseball with lead offs, stealing and running on passed balls. New to all of our players, but second nature to the club teams we would be playing.

During another game, our other newbie caught three pop ups in left field. He got a game ball for that. I don't think I've ever seen a kid who never played before catch three fly balls in one day. That he couldn't hit meant nothing.

We worked daily with our pitchers. Most were capable of giving us a good 1/3 of an inning, but yes, I could see improvement during practice. I don't think anyone else saw the improvement. We just kept working, and the kids never lost faith. We wouldn't dwell on our loses nor the scores. We offered encouragement for good at bats, good innings, and good (well, maybe not good, just not bad) plays.

When football season and cross country ended, we actually had a couple of practices where we had all of our players. It came the week before the league tournament was to start. And yes, we had our best practices of the year. The kids had fun, and we didn't even talk about the upcoming tournament or who we were going to play. We just had fun at practice and kept working.

As usual we played our one strike game and the line game. We offered an incentive to the winner of the one strike game: naming the field after the winner.

As we started our league tournament, we certainly didn't scare anyone. We had a 1-9-1 record in a 17 team league. We had given up 119 runs (the worst in the league) and scored only 29 (you guessed it, the worst in the league).

The big day finally came. We started our tournament. Miracles of miracles, we surprised everyone and eked out a win in our first game. Luck, pure luck.

When we won our second game, no one but our coaches and our players believed it. Maybe they didn't either, but here we were, playing for the championship of our division!! And without our most talented player (his parents chose to have him play in a league soccer game rather than for a baseball championship).

We played well and competed well, but were down 3 in the 7th and last inning with two outs, at the bottom of our order. Under our league rules, we could hit all 10 of our players. That meant we had a number of almost automatic outs. Our hope against hope was to somehow turn over the lineup and get back to the top of the order before we accumulated three outs.

When our number 10 hitter (down to his last strike with two outs) hit his hardest ball of the year which was biffed by the opposing shortstop, we still had a life. Our lead-off hitter, Mychal, was our best hitter. With two strikes, he doubled. Runners on second and third with two outs. Down 2. Up came grandson Brandon. Down to our last strike again, he singled and tied up the game. Up came third baseman Chase who also went to two strikes. As he did so, Brandon stole second and third. Chase then got a base hit to put us in the lead.

Our last 8 hitters went to two strikes. Two more hitters followed up with two strike base hits as we went up two. And that's how the game ended.

After the third out in the bottom of the seventh, our kids and their parents went absolutely crazy. You would have thought we won the world series. It was something those kids will never forget. How improbable was that victory!

Patience and the one strike game paid off. Though we were the least likely team to win a championship, these kids were used to being up with the equivalence of two strikes every single day. No panic. Absolutely no panic.

We were then scheduled to play another tournament the following weekend. Improbably we continued to win. In the championship game we were in almost the same spot as the previous week. This time, in extra innings with the bases loaded and two out, the same cast of characters took charge. This time, Brandon won it with a base hit.

The kids were the talk of their school. Later on during Grandparents' day at the school, a number of the teachers made note of our kids' success.

Quite the feather in their caps. Patience paid off.

Yes, they sure did improve. During our first 10 games, we did not throw a runner out stealing. During our last 6 games we threw out 8 runners.

When asked how he improved so much Mychal, our catcher, had a simple answer. "Coach trusted me."

Don't wait for a kid to face real pressure before putting him on the field. If he strikes out with the bases loaded during the season (even if it costs you a game), at least he'll have been put in the position to perform when he is needed (as he almost assuredly will be).

Sometimes you have to lose early, to win later. Just trust the kids.

Chapter 5

Playing To Win

Playing to win has a number of meanings. We try not to let the idea of winning get in the way of winning. What exactly does that mean? Let me explain.

Like most of life, the bottom line is ever important. But, sometimes winning is more than the final score. Sometimes winning means more than that. This is something a coach should always remember. It is really why we play the game.

This was brought home to us when my son, Rusty, played Senior League Baseball for a local Little League. We had a powerhouse team along with some of the best players in the league, but which included Steve the **least** talented player in the league.

He was one of those kids who would literally run through walls for his team. And yes, he did so. I'll never forget him running through a cyclone fence after a ball, or standing on home plate to get hit so he could get on base for his team.

Our group won dozens of games playing together in the Tucson Summer, Fall and Winter leagues. We were ordered by the league to take Steve. Even with him, our winning streak was well into double figures. The streak continued until our very last game against our biggest rivals. There was no love lost between the two teams. We could not lose to these guys!

We played terrible ball, and were behind going into the bottom of the 7th, and last inning. Rusty and Jeff (whose Dad had played for John Wooden at UCLA during their 1964 National Basketball Championship campaign), a future 5th round MLB draft pick (and now a lawyer in Phoenix) were on the bench. They were terrific hitters.

One of them would win the game for sure. They each grabbed bats, swinging them in such a way that I would be sure to notice them. Down 1, we had the tying run on third and the winning run on second with Steve at bat. Surely, rather than lose the game, the dumb coach, me, would re-enter one of our stars who would get up there and win the game for us.

Rusty and Jeff could not believe that I was not going to put them in. They visibly cringed when I told Steve to get a bat.

Steve did not have even one hit the entire season, not one. I'm not even sure he hit a fair ball! In our batting practice before the final game, I had him bat first, third, fifth, seventh and ninth and vowed if I couldn't get him a hit, I'd quit coaching. And yes, I was totally serious. As he moved to the plate, our players looked daggers at me. If looks could kill.

They knew I was nuts, and was just throwing away the game. It sure looked like my retirement from coaching was imminent. They were furious, as were the parents.

Well, Steve got up to bat and looked horrible on the first pitch. Strike one!! The fans and players of both teams knew the game would be over with Steve's fourth strikeout of the game. The next pitch, Strike 2. Why wouldn't that dumb Coach let Rusty or Jeff hit? Did I want to lose that badly? What was wrong with me! We just couldn't lose to these guys.

Next pitch, swing, and a foul ball (barely), in and out of the catcher's glove. Whew, that was close. Surely I'd make the change now. No, stubborn to the last. Even I could not watch.

The next pitch, Steve swung and lofted a short fly ball toward right field, the first baseman gave chase, the second baseman took an angle to the ball, and the right fielder came hard. Each dove, and the ball dropped between them. The runners on third and second scored. Steve was safe at first. We won!

The kids carried Steve off the field. His parents came and thanked me with tears in their eyes (truthfully they weren't the only ones). For one exquisite moment that will live for his whole life, Steve was a hero, a Champion.

The look of pride on the faces of his Mom and Dad was worth everything.

I don't know where Steve is, or what he is doing, but I know that moment will live with him forever.

Rusty wrote an Article about this game that was published in *Guideposts* Magazine, and won himself a small college scholarship. He called it "Playing to Win."

Playing to win means a lot of things. For Steve, it was more than a win.

Chapter 6

Un-Coaching

Over the years I have gotten criticized for rarely giving signs from the third base coaching box. That is true. At the youth level (actually at any level) I believe it is a sign of failure to need to give a bunch of signs.

I want my kids to know what to do, and when to do it. Why give a bunt sign with a runner on and nobody out late in the game with the score tied and the third baseman back? Shouldn't our player know enough to do what is needed? If not, what have I been teaching?

A lot of what we do is what I call un-coaching. We work very hard, and take pride in how hard we work. I always told our kids we were the hardest working team in Arizona if not the world. Our goal: to have the kids "play" ball. We don't want them to submerge their instincts. Base coaches, as Pete Rose always said are "there to help us, not own us."

Good base runners know where the ball is, what the situation is, and need to learn when to run. Looking for the approval of the base coach makes them hesitate. It takes time for players to learn this because it is foreign to most of them. And yes, they often will be thrown out. Learning what not to do by doing.

With a runner on first and a single to right, we want our runner to end up at third most of the time. They do that by using their instincts and running like hell. Stutter steps and extra looks at the base coach won't help them get there any faster. In fact, uncertainty slows a runner down.

If they know where the ball is, and where the fielder is, their basic instincts (and having been through the situation hundreds of times before) will generally propel them in the right direction and in making the correct decision.

Sure, they'll get thrown out at times, but once they unlearn what they have been taught and learn to hustle through their instincts, they will, more often than not, make the right decision. When they are unsuccessful, we blame the coach ("the Coach is an idiot"). When successful, they get the glory. Of course, the parents always blame the coach, which is ok too. It takes the pressure off the kids.

It is our philosophy to always score from second on a base hit. That means the player must be ready and know instinctively what to do.

Baseball players need to have the freedom and permission to make mistakes. That's how they learn. They need to be free to make mistakes, not programmed to worry. They need the freedom. After all, most of the kids have played ball for years and years.

Here's an example. We were playing in a Legion game against one of our biggest rivals with a future major leaguer on the mound. The game was tight all the way. In the 9th, our shortstop was on second base with one out. The hitter hit a ball toward first base with the pitcher covering. The runner from second set out as the ball was hit.

The pitcher, Tom Wilhelmson (who later became the Seattle Mariner's closer) made the putout at first, and threw hurriedly to home, a 93 mile per hour strike. The umpire called the runner out at home (I still maintain that he was safe, and will go to my grave with that belief).

A number of parents and players were angry with me because they felt I should not have sent the runner (though the truth was, he went on his own). I did not bark at the runner, but instead, congratulated him on his hustle.

A couple of weeks later, under almost the same situation our runner scored from second on a ground ball to second, winning us the Arizona State American Legion Championship, 1-0. Had I gotten on the runner the previous time, our runner would have hesitated before taking the chance. I'm totally glad he did not hesitate!!!

When we have runners on second and third with one or no outs, we always run our runner from third on a ground ball. No matter where or to whom it is directed.

That really sounds foolish, doesn't it? I've certainly been told that many times by detractors. But there is really a method to the craziness.

If there are runners on second and third, and a ball is hit to the pitcher, why let them get an easy out at first, making the situation runners on second and third with one out. Instead, I run the runner from third. The hitter's job is to get as far as he can if the ball is not thrown to first. The job of the runner on third is to attempt to score, but if the ball beats him home, he is to stop (we "never, ever, never, ever, run into a tag"), turn and run back to third. The runner on second under those circumstances is to get to and stop at third (don't make the mistake of running back to second and end up in a double play).

While the runner from third is turning and running back to third, the hitter is hauling his butt toward second. If the ball is thrown, and beats him, he is to stop and get in a pickle so the runner from third can try and score.

If the fielder then throws home, the worst that can happen is that our runner from third is out and we have the same situation, runners at second and third with one out, but have had a lot more fun than simply letting the pitcher throw our hitter out. We still have runners on second and third, and have made the defense work for what should have been a simple out. Sometimes when the runner is on his way to second, we've even been known to have him fall down, seemingly helpless. That adds in the deception.

So, even when it doesn't work, we end up in exactly the same position we would have been in had we not run the runners from second and third, and just let them throw to first base for the easy out.

But, even then, we've had way more fun than if we simply played it conservatively and let them get us out. And we've given them a whole slew of opportunities to make mistakes and throw the ball away. Sometimes teams are so used to going to first on such a play that they simply do so. Meanwhile, we have stolen a run.

Most teams do not execute first and third plays very well. So we often try and give them the opportunity to make a play. For example, with a runner on third and ball four to our hitter, our hitter will simply keep running. When he reaches first, we are now in a typical first and third situation. The runner will keep going toward second.

The runner from third will score if the catcher or pitcher throws to second to stop the just walked runner. Once again if the ball beats our runner, he'll get in a pickle. It's amazing how many teams can't seem to execute a simple pickle play, even at higher levels of baseball. When the ball is thrown to get the pickled guy out, our runner from third will try and score. The infield is usually not ready to cut the ball off as they do in regular first and third situations, so a throw to second almost always scores the runner.

That does not mean we don't outsmart ourselves on occasion either. One year coaching a local Junior Varsity team, we were getting ready to play one of our big rivals and worked on one specific first and third play during the four practice days we had prior to playing them. The guys we were playing were ultra aggressive on the base paths.

Almost always they would run an early break from first to try and score the runner from third. Our play was to simply have the pitcher step off, and make a full fake throw to second with both of our infielders breaking for the bag. After the fake, he was to turn throw the ball to third to catch that runner anticipating the throw to second. We practiced the play at least 100 times to perfection.

Sure enough, we had our first and third situation very early in the game. The runner from first left early, and our pitcher turned for the fake. The runner on third took the bait and broke for home. He was caught in no man's land and was clearly dead meat. Except that our pitcher, instead of faking, forgot the play and threw the ball into center field, allowing both runners to score.

Boy was I a lousy coach. Why in heavens name did I have my pitcher throw the ball? Yes, the coach was an idiot, just as advertised.

I hate leaving runners at third, and my players know it (and so it turns out do most of our opponents). That's why we take scoring leads from second every single time we are on second (unless we intend to steal third in which case a straight line lead is in order). Our goal is to score. Shouldn't that be everyone's goal?

We never tell a kid to "freeze" on a line drive. If you freeze, and a liner is caught, you are out, pure and simple. The infielders are all moving to the liner and to cover the base. If you freeze, you have no chance. On the other hand, if you think it will be caught, haul butt back. At least you'll have a chance to be safe.

You won't if you "freeze." Plus, if you freeze and the ball goes through, you've also lost your chance to score. The player has the right, under our system to be wrong. If he hustles back and the liner is through, that's baseball. If he breaks for home thinking the ball is through and a play is made, oh, well, that's baseball as well.

On the other hand, if you think it is through, run like a mad man and score. If you are wrong, so be it. I tell my kids when their Dad is on them about not "freezing on a line drive" to blame me. Coach is an idiot. If they are safe and score, then feel free to take the credit of being aggressive on the base paths. More often than not, the player makes the correct move. In any season we score more than we give up by being aggressive.

The truth is, freezing is not, and never has been successful on a ball field, though I can't tell you how many times I've heard good baseball folks yell at the players to "freeze". And criticize my players for not freezing.

The moral of the story: don't freeze, do something. Something your instinct and experience tells you to do. If you depend on the base coach, by the time you hear and process what he has to say, you're out. I tell the kids, "if you are on base and a ball is hit to the outfield and you think it will be down, run. If you are wrong, it's the coaches fault. If you are right, you're a hero. Don't be afraid to be a hero.

Fear, like freezing, has no place on a ball field.

Chapter 7

It's About Who is Here,
Not Who Is Missing

You win by playing the game as best you can. Don't worry who you are playing or which of your players are at the game.

A number of years ago I was coaching my KFC American Legion team. We had a terrific squad, but were on the cusp of elimination from local, State and Regional play. Because of monsoon rain outs (common in Tucson during the summer), we had to play and win 4 double headers in four days to advance. But, worse than that, our first baseman who hit a record number of home runs for us, left us for a job with a magazine.

Our second baseman a future D-1 player, whose Dad was the football coach at Pima Community College and is now the Athletic Director, left us for preseason high school football and our third baseman, a member of the United States Junior National team was not allowed to play because of misbehavior to his Guardian.

That left us with but nine players. Our new first baseman was a guy who had never started a high school baseball game (even on senior day). He had the game winning RBI in the Arizona State Championship game.

Our new second baseman was a junior varsity player, and hit a three run homer (the only home run of his entire life) against Taylorsville, Utah, to ignite us. He circled the bases jumping and skipping the whole way.

"I just hit the only home run of my life," he was yelling. Even the Taylorsville players smiled as he rounded the bases (he was the front page of the Salt Lake Tribune the next day, in living color).

Our new third baseman was also a junior varsity player who scored the winning run in State from second on a fielders choice ground ball to second.

To make matters worse, our corner outfielders were PO's (pitchers only). Players who rarely if ever got to bat for their high schools. How could we win with that crew?

Yet win we did!

Eight straight in four days to qualify for the post season. Five more in four days to get to State, and four more in four days to qualify for the West Region in Utah as state champions.

Even worse than that, in the West Regional we were playing those odds on favorites from Taylorsville, Utah, who would be starting the Utah player of the year, who was drafted in the top five rounds of the MLB draft. We were indeed, in trouble.

To get to the Regionals, our iron nine played stellar ball, knocking off team after team, and winning the championship when our left fielder, Jamie, (a future major leaguer) pitched a no hitter.

Tied in the last inning Jamie came off the field and announced that he knew we'd score, and that if the game went twenty more innings, they wouldn't score a run.

With runners on first and second with one out, our first baseman hit a fielder's choice ground ball to the second baseman's right.

As the second baseman moved to field the ball, our third baseman, who was on second, took off at contact. When the ball was thrown to first for the out, the runner never hesitated, and continued running, beating the throw home for a State Championship. We were on our way to Ogden.

To this day, nineteen years later when I see Skip, our third baseman (now a Fire Captain in a local fire department), he asks whether or not I sent him. I just shrug and smile.

We arrived in Ogden, our crew of 11 (10 players-we got a sub back who couldn't come to State-plus me). When we entered the initial welcoming meeting it was clear we were in over our heads.

The tournament director called the role. California-18 players, five coaches and 21 fan rooms; Hawaii, 17 players 3 coaches, 17 fans; Utah 18 players, 4 coaches, and so it went until we were called. Arizona: 10 players, one coach and one fan.

"You came to Regionals with only 10 players?" "Yes, sir."

"Can't come to Regionals with just 10 players!" "Why not, did you change the rules?"

"What do you mean?"

"I mean. we only need nine to play. We had nine for our state tournament, and have 10 now, so we think we're loaded. And, I'll tell you what, if we don't give a good account for ourselves, I'll never bring another team to Regionals again."

They actually did change the rules for later years in response to me, by requiring a team to have no fewer than 12 players).

"Well, who will pitch for you?"

"Easy, our right fielder will pitch the first game, the guy who played right field in the first game will pitch the second one, and our left fielder (who later made it to the major leagues as a pitcher) will pitch the third. After that we'll go with our shortstop and center fielder."

The organizers gave us a time for using a local field for batting practice and working out. When we got to the field we noticed that the team we would be playing the following night was hiding on a hill watching us, so we gave them something to see. All our batters batted the opposite way, our fielders threw with their wrong hands. We made the Bad News Bears look like super stars.

The next morning the papers couldn't say enough bad things about us. We were making a mockery of the Regional Tournament, we would be blown out by the great Taylorsville team, winners of a couple of million in a row. Even the Taylorsville players got their swipes in ("they don't really look like ballplayers").

Our guys were unfazed. They took the same attitude into the Taylorsville game that they took when they basically needed to win 17 in a row to get to Regionals.

We were the designated home team. Our pitcher went out in the first inning and on the first pitch gave up a monster home run. The second guy hit a rocket off the left field wall of the beautiful retro Ogden field (it actually was a wall) for a double. Things looked pretty bleak. I went out to talk to our pitcher.

"What am I going to do, Coach?" he asked.

Here's what I said to our lefty: "Well, Jim, all I can say is that you are throwing too damn hard. I want you to throw nothing but slow curves for a while and see how that works. After all, if you can't throw 94 throw 49."

So that was what he did. Six curves and three pop outs later and we were out of the inning. His offerings barely registered on the scoreboard speed gun.

As the game went on, the frustrated Utah team swung harder and harder and popped higher and higher as my pitcher threw slower and slower. I took more and more abuse from the Utah dugout as I stood in the third base coaching box with my score book in hand.

"You're pitching a grammar school kid!" They also assailed my intelligence as well as my looks and ethnicity.

I couldn't believe the names and insults sent my way. Through it all, I had my pitcher stay the course.

When we got up to bat in the first inning I gathered our players and told them we would score nine runs, and the final run would be a suicide squeeze. And that's exactly what we did.

It included a home run by our JV second baseman who ran around the field in ecstacy, jumping up and down yelling, "I hit my first home run, I hit my first home run...."

Everyone in the park smiled at his exuberance and excitement (even the guys from Taylorsville). And it wasn't like he hit his home run off someone who couldn't throw. This kid had D-1, high minor's stuff and was drafted in the 5th round by the Twins.

Our home run hitter was the front page (in color) of the Salt Lake Tribune the next morning.

Yes, kids step up when you give them a shot.

By the way, Jimmie struck out the last three hitters of the game by throwing three fast balls, 89, 90, and 91. They weren't ready for that. After that, the Coach looked at me differently.

Our guys just didn't know they weren't that talented. They weren't worried about who we were missing. They were a team that lived and died together. They truly enjoyed the experience and playing together.

They even became the most popular kids in Utah after beating dreaded Taylorsville, They even stood up on the dugout during one of the other games doing the YMCA song, complete with arm motions.

As usual for our team, by Tournament's end, the tournament committee had no derogatory words for our team which lost the championship to a powerhouse California team that won the American Legion World Series the next week.

Playing and trusting your kids makes a huge difference.

When we needed a catcher for our team, I approached a local high school coach. He tried to talk me out of bringing on his high school catcher. He said, "you just don't want Bubby. Here, let me show you."

He took me over to the batting cage. "You see that monster dent in the batting cage pole? Bubby!" He then pointed out another dent. "Bubby!" And another: "Bubby!"

I got the message, but dumb as a stump, I took Bubby anyway. One of the best decisions ever. The kid loved to catch, back to back games, double headers, 110 degrees, no matter. He loved it. He loved the game. Never a complaint. Oh, sure, he was very hard on himself. He would get on himself when he struck out. But you never saw a more loyal, or a better teammate anywhere.

When we recruited players to our KFC Legion team I had one major requirement: to play for us they had to love it, and be willing to play anywhere on the field.

And they had to be approved by the other players. Most everyone we had loved playing for us. Even today, I can't go anywhere in town without being met by former players who remember KFC baseball as the most fun they ever had playing ball.

Sometimes you just trust the player and your instincts.

For another example. I usually did not allow undergraduates to play for us. I felt they needed to play for their high school summer teams, unless there was no team, or the player was not welcome. I did not want to interfere with their high school program. One day the Coach of a local high school (one where I had been an assistant) called me.

"Alex," he said. "Could you do me a really big favor, a really big favor?"

"Sure, Mark, what is it."

"I have a player that isn't a graduating senior, and he just drives me crazy. I just can't stand to have him around. Could you get this kid off my back for the summer?"

As usual, in keeping with my philosophy that "fools walk in where angels fear to tread." I took the kid. He didn't really like it when I changed him from third base to center field, but he really wanted to play.

Surprisingly, to most people, he became the best 6'8" center fielder we ever had (we actually did have another who was also very good). He loved playing with our guys, and like Bubby, was a great teammate. Even today, Brad is one of our most loyal KFC alumni ever.

Here's another example of our philosophy and trust in our players from the words of a former player, and current college head coach talking about us playing an All Star Academy team in a tournament with only nine players on our roster:

"We went through pool play and made it to the playoff portion in which they matched us up with the powerful Albuquerque Baseball Academy (ABA) even though we were clearly the top 2 teams in the tournament.

They were purposely not taxed at all during the first part of the tournament, and had all of their pitching left. I started and gave up a 5 spot in the first inning. They were hitting everything I threw up there.

We faced 3 guys over 90 including a guy who got it up to 96 mph that day. In the bottom of the first, we had 2 guys get on base and Seth Mejias-Breen [Recently called up to the Padres] hit a 3 run home run to steady us. I proceeded to throw 4 shutout innings to get us into the 6th inning, getting ground ball after ground ball.

We then continued to battle and took an 8-5 lead. Will Holbrook warmed up every single inning from the 1st into the 6th and finally came on to close it out. He ended up getting the save and we advanced to the Semi's.

The thing that struck me most about you personally that day was that you had a really long leash and trusted me. You came out and basically asked me if I thought I had it that day.

And I said yes but to keep warming up Holbrook because I had a lot of faith in him. You sticking with me that long and us continuing to be confident and the KFC mind set that we are going to beat anybody we play ended up being the difference in the game.

Seth had a monster day that day and our team battled. That was the first time we had beaten ABA since I had been there after losing in the championship the year prior (we ran out of pitching for that game)."

Chapter 8

It's About The Kids, It Really Is

We hear this all the time about youth baseball. "It's for the kids! It's for the kids!"

But is it really? Let's face it, its usually for the local Little League, Legion, Connie Mack or high school coaches "in group," or an ego group wanting to show the world how they can recruit the best and most talented kids in town and sometimes out of town (sometimes it's the same people).

The game should be for the kids, but most of the time, sorrowfully, it is not. There are amazing, hidden benefits when it really is for the kids.

Stupid rules, administrators who believe they are the lords of their fiefdoms, parents who make everybody's life miserable, and umpires who are in it for the money, or their egos, only conspire to subvert the ideal.

These groups begin recruiting kids to play as young as eight years old. And who do they recruit? Their buddies' kids, and the biggest, most mature kids they can find from the most well to do families. That leaves behind untold thousands of kids (and parents) who are spurned and turned off from the game.

I married a woman whose boys were neglected in Little Leagues, and never got to play as much as they deserved. Josh didn't make an All Star team until he was 14 in senior league. Even then, he sat the bench mostly. Unjustifiably to our mind.

When we decided to put together a team to beat their league all stars, he got his chance, and became our 105 pound catcher [he's now 6' 180 and all muscle]. When given a chance, all he did was improve. So much so, that as a senior in high school he was the first team catcher on the Southern Arizona All Region team. His next stop was junior college baseball.

Josh was the energizer bunny personified. After working a full day outside in over 100 degree weather at a local nursery, he rushed to our evening double header. He got there in time to put on the gear.

He caught every inning of the double header. We were playing at a major league spring training complex of four fields in a circle around an observation building. A number of balls were hit over the backstop into the building which was locked.

A ball was popped up the first base line. Josh gave chase, dove and caught the ball. He dropped his glove and equipment, ran out the gate of the first base dugout, jumped on the fence and climbed up the building. At the top he threw a few balls down to the field, jumped down, ran to the dugout, grabbed a bat and led off the inning. You just can't beat energy and desire.

Darn it, it needs to be about the players. Give them a chance. While my teams are not democracies, the players actually have a say in what goes on. And that starts when the kids are 8 or 9. Give the kids credit for having sense. They will surprise you.

Most Little Leagues don't let the kids pick their own All Star team. It is usually done by parents who claim that the kids would simply pick their friends. That is really not true. In actuality the kids do a better job at picking teams than the adults do. The adults all pick their favorites (or the league president's son) according to the politics of the league.

Against the advice of the league "know it alls," one year we took a group of 9 going on 10 years olds into our local winter league. "You can't do that the people said!" But we did. The league was basically an 11 and 12 year old league. "Your kids will get killed!!!

Yes, we were, by far, the youngest, and smallest kids you've ever seen. As expected, we lost our first 4 games, and wondered whether or not we'd ever win a game! Had we actually bitten off more than we could chew? Were the nay sayers really right this time? I even had to tell our coaches not to give up hope.

Our most talented player was, to put it mildly, a brat. But he was our best. He was our best fielder, hitter and pitcher, and by quite a large margin. He'd been warned a couple of times about his behavior, and the last straw was when he missed practice, and we could see him watching us from a vantage point some distance away. I had had it. The kids were even angrier. Enough was enough.

I called the kids in for a meeting and told them that this was their team, and what they decided was what we would do. I reviewed the situation and told them that I was planning to throw Danny off the team, but that I wanted their input before doing so.

I would not do so if they didn't want me to. After they huddled together (without our interference), they came back with their verdict. To a "man" they felt that Danny was not someone they wanted on their team, that he was "mean", and selfish, and even if they lost every game it would be more fun without him.

So we kicked him off the team, and began winning. Sometimes we would say, less is more. We won 14 straight, as a matter of fact. It was their team, and they were proud. They made a decision together, and were prepared for the consequences. They also learned something too, as did we. Pay attention, sometimes the youngest among us are wise beyond their years. It pays to listen and respect their feelings and opinions.

In putting our teams together, we would take kids, regardless of size. Our goal: to get kids with hustle and heart, to us, the two most under-rated attributes of a ball player. As an example, a number of years ago I watched a very, very small kid play against us. He was too small to hit the ball out of a Little League infield. But boy did he hustle. After the game was over, I grabbed him and told him he could play on my team any time. Any time!!!

Johnny ended up playing for us often. And though he would never be a big kid, when he started to mature he lifted weights like a mad man to gain the strength he needed to compete. As a freshman he tried out for his high school team and was cut. Did that dissuade him? No sirreebob!. That just made him work even harder. But still, he was cut as a soph. And yet, he persisted.

He made the squad as a Junior, though he played on the junior varsity team most of the time. He went out again as a senior, and this time he stuck, and started most games.

He played on our fall team that year. During one particular game he led off the game by doubling over the left fielder's head (it seems that if you are small, no one thinks you can hit despite all of the evidence to the contrary).

The next time he was up the coach yelled to the outfield to play deeper. They did. Once again he hit it over the left fielder's head.

For his next at bat, the coach yelled to his players that if Johnny hit it over their heads again, they would watch the rest of the game from the bench. So what did Johnny do? He hit it over their heads, but he also hit it over the fence, so there was nothing they could do.

Johnny, Josh, and our pitcher Brit went up to Yavapai College in Prescott, Arizona for a tryout. The results of the tryout were disappointing. Johnny was rated as too small, Josh was rated as too small with not enough power and Brit didn't throw hard enough. "Average high school players" was how they were rated.

They went up to Yavapai with such promise, only to have their feelings crushed.

As luck (or actually the baseball gods) would have it, we played the actual Yavapai superstar recruits in the semifinals of the High Desert Classic in Albuquerque. Johnny played left, Josh caught, and Brit pitched. They all made sure the opposing coach knew they were "the average high school players" he rejected. Johnny opened the game with a homer, Josh threw out the first runner trying to steal, and Brit struck out the side in the very first inning.

There was no let up as we mercy ruled those guys. Brit later played D-1 ball, was drafted, and later coached at both the high school and junior college level. Josh played JC ball, and as to Johnny, upon graduation from high school he decided that he would go to Notre Dame and walk on. Once again he was cut as a freshman. He went to the coach and asked what he needed to do to stick. He worked even harder. His second year he was cut again. Still he persisted.

As a perennial Dean's list member with a 3.56 average, he tried again as a junior, and guess what? He made the team. He was a real life Rudy. He wasn't a starter, but exulted on those times when he got to play.

The highlight of the season was against St. John's. Johnny had his chance. He pinch hit late in the game, and had the game winning RBI. Amazingly, his game winning hit resulted in Notre Dame reaching the number 1 spot in the Collegiate Baseball weekly baseball poll for the first time ever.

John, today is a happy and successful lawyer.

Through the years, when I would put a team together, the players were the final arbiters of who would play with us. One year they rejected a player who had been drafted by the Rangers because the kids didn't feel he would help chemistry. "We want this to be a fun team, Coach." The next year after he grew up a little they asked me to invite him to play with us.

Another year they made what I thought was one of the most amazing decisions I ever had a group make.

We were playing a game at the University of Arizona when an accented Hispanic young man, Adolpho, came up to me and asked if he could play for us. I asked where he went to school. He told me he went to the University and was a senior, graduating in December. I told him he had to be too old.

"No," he said, "I'm 18" He really was. It seems he was born and grew up in Mexico. Because his parents had to work, he was sent to school with his older sister who was about three years older. He paid attention, and as a result, he was way ahead grade wise of the other kids he knew. When his family came to the United States, he was at least three grade levels above his contemporaries.

Because geography matters in Legion baseball which has all kinds of technical rules, I asked where he lived. He lived near Sahuaro High School, my base school at the time. I then asked where he went to high school, and that became the rub. He had gone to high school in Denver, graduating at 12 ½. Because he went to that high school, under American Legion Rules, we had to pick up the enrollment for that school which, when added to our total enrollment from the schools represented on our team, put us well over the 5,000 maximum allowed by Legion and would make us an illegally constituted team. He told me he was a pitcher, so I went out to the bullpen with our catcher and Adolpho.

He warmed up, and threw some for us. It was clear, he wasn't going to be a superstar, but he was a really nice kid, and could certainly earn some innings with us from the right side. After watching him throw, I looked at his glove which was a weird six fingered glove. I asked him about it. His mother made it for him, he said, so he could put it on either of his hands.

He changed the glove and put it on his right hand instead of his left, and threw a couple of pitches lefty. I couldn't see any real difference whether he threw lefty or right. From that time on, he was "Ambi" (for ambidextrous). I told him he could play in some of our non-Legion games (we also played in our local Connie Mack League which had no attendance limitations and way fewer rules than did Legion ball).

So he began playing with us. Sometimes he threw left, and sometimes he threw right. Sometimes both in the same inning, and once to the same batter.

As we got closer to the start of our local Area A legion league, I spoke with Bud, our Area A Chairman, thinking that perhaps we could get a waiver, since the kid was too young to play varsity baseball when he was in high school, and it didn't seem to give us an unfair advantage over other teams.

Bud, our Area A Chairman, thought we had a very good case for a waiver, since, after all, the rules "should be all about the kids...."

He cautioned, that it could take some time for Indianapolis to make a decision (as it did), and if he played any Legion games for us, they could end up as forfeits should the ruling later go against us.

He opined that he thought we would have a very good case for a waiver, however, and that he was in favor of it.

I spoke with the kids for their input. I told them what was at stake. If he played and was later ruled to be ineligible we would forfeit all of our victories, and would not get back to State again (we were defending state champions). The players knew we were really good, but decided:

"'Ambi' is one of us, and we win or lose together. If we win the league and he is found to be ineligible, that would be sad, but it's a risk we're willing to take for a teammate."

I don't know if I've ever been so proud of a group of kids. As it turned out, we were by far the best team in Area A that season. We went on to win 18 league games.

When Legion denied the waiver near the end of the season in rather insulting fashion claiming we stock piled University of Arizona players (untrue, though Coach Lopez' son, David was a great player for us one year). We forfeited all our wins, and didn't get to defend our state championship title. Yes, our guys were disappointed, but it was a decision they made, lived with and died with for a teammate. Yes, there are many benefits when we play the game for the kids.

That year, 2001, when we were ineligible to play, was the very last time a team from Phoenix area Legion beat a Tucson team to advance to the West Regional tournament.

How proud could someone be of their players. Yes, there are a number of ways to win. These guys were, to my mind, true winners.

Chapter 9

Teaching Without Really Teaching

A. The One Strike Game

One of the really great ways of teaching is by putting the kids in a position where they are learning, but don't realize they are being taught.

There are many ways to coach: through the use of video, repetition, demonstration, have them do it, and finally, here is another way, trick them into learning.

Our hitting philosophy is simple. Every coach in America wants his pitcher to throw a first pitch fastball for a strike. At every level of baseball the first pitch is a fast ball at least 80% of the time. That being the case, we teach our kids to look for it. To "look for that pitch to kill." How do we teach this?

By inventing a series of games using their basic competitiveness.

For example, the one strike game (which was mentioned earlier in this manuscript). The kids line up with their helmets on in a line. They each get to take but one swing. If they swing at a bad pitch they are eliminated. If they take a fast ball down the gut, they are eliminated, swing and miss they are eliminated.

Hit a foul ball, you guessed it, they are eliminated, except that if they make contact in the first round only, they get to stay in. No one wants to lose, so as they play the game they take fewer and fewer strikes down the hole, and swing at fewer and fewer bad pitches. It is a badge of honor on our team to win the game. They really go at it.

By the end of the season, you don't see our teams swing at many bad ones. It helps save my lungs. You won't hear me yelling much at our guys to "lay off the high ones" or some such. They go up with nothing on their minds but to look for that pitch to kill.

That's how they win at the one strike game, that's how they win in real ball games. The idea is to put as much pressure put on the kids in the one strike game as they will ever get in a real game. And believe me, they take it seriously.

The last two standing become captains for another game that we play called the line game. More about that later.

The One Strike Game reinforces our philosophy. I try to keep them aggressive, and never will they hear me tell them to "protect," even with two strikes. My refrain, "look for a pitch to kill." Why get defensive now!!! If we are going to make an out, we'll go down swinging. We play many other games which will be discussed later.

That's why we were not surprised when batter after batter was unfazed going to two strikes on our Pride team. To our players, hitting with two strikes is what they are used to doing, so why is everybody so surprised that we hit with two strikes?

B. The Line Game: You Can Too Teach Hustle!

Nothing makes me sicker than to watch teams (my team included), at any level, meander on and off the field. Nothing tells more about the respect your kids have been taught for the game than how they enter or leave the field.

Of course, there is the old adage that it takes no talent to hustle. I often tell our players that if you hustle on the field with enthusiasm you are more apt to make a play, and that when you hustle off the field you are more apt to get a hit.

We also tell our kids that there are things you do for yourself, things you do for your parents, things you do for your coaches, and things you do to avoid penalties, such as doing extra running.

Sometimes these things work, sometimes they work for a little while, and somctimes they don't.

Our solution is to devise games that require hustle in order to compete. How do you do that, you say? Pretty simple. Invent a game that requires hustle as one of the rules of the game.

When we play the one strike game, invented primarily to force the players to be aggressive in the strike zone, and to be aggressive with only one more strike left, to be unafraid of two strike panic, and indeed to learn the zone, we add a couple of elements.

One batter after another jumps into the box. There is absolutely no hesitation before the next pitch is thrown. That means players must hop in and out immediately. If they do not, a pitch is thrown and they are out, eliminated from competition.

Upon elimination they have to get on the field to shag within eight seconds-if they do not, they can't compete in the next game. Truly, any kid that has ever laced on spikes hates to shag, but hates missing a turn at bat more!

The two winners of the one strike game then get to choose teams for the next game: the line game. Barriers, usually cones, but sometimes gloves, catcher's gear, sometimes even a player's younger brother or anything else loose are placed on the field on either side of second base to give a funnel like area the hitter must hit into. It's basically a hit up the middle game. The more players we have, the wider the barriers, the fewer, the narrower.

The rules are simple. A hitter gets up to bat and, must try and hit the ball up the middle. Two foul balls (any ball hit outside the barriers) is an out. Any caught pop up is an out, any swing and miss is an out. Any infield ground ball kept in front of an infielder before touching the outfield grass is an out. Any ball through a players legs anywhere on the field in fair territory is an automatic home run. A dropped pop up is a double if in the infield, a triple if in the outfield. A base hit up the middle is a base hit. Any ball hit over the head of the last outfielder is a home run, as is any ball over the fence in fair territory.

Now comes the hustle part.

There is no base running in this game.

But, after a hitter, there is no hesitation. The next hitter must be in position with his helmet on immediately. The old pitching machine (me) waits for no one. If the next hitter isn't in the box immediately, a ball will be thrown, and he's out.

Each batter must quickly follow another, or the side is retired. When the side is retired (three outs or one lack of hustle), the team on the field must get all of its players off the field and a batter up, within 10 seconds. If they do not, the side is automatically retired. Lord help the player that causes his teammates to lose their at bats.

The team heading for the field must get there before the team exiting the field gets a batter to the plate. If the team is not on the field and a ball is hit, it's an automatic home run.

Nothing angers a ball player more than when one of his teammates does not hustle on or off the field and it costs his team a run, or their time at bat.

We often play a nine inning line game in under ten minutes. When we are done, equipment is strewn everywhere. Usually its best two out of three. Loser cleans up.

It is really neat to watch these kids running on and off, hustling everywhere. Since we usually do this toward the end of practice, parents are usually on the sidelines exhorting their kids on. After a time, hustle becomes a part of their lives.

Did I mention, that the kids love it. One of my teams tried to get the City of Tucson to allow them to play a 24 hour line game for charity. Alas, the city fathers rejected our request.

We try to add competition at every stage of practice.

C. Helter Skelter

Another of our games is called Helter-Skelter.

For our younger kids, we set practice to start either on the hour, or half hour. If they arrive early they have at least fifteen minutes to play various games before the full team arrives. One of our games is the old game of hit the bat. This gets them ready to play Helter Skelter. In Hit the Bat the player gets up with a ball and bat and hits the ball out of his hand. The players on the field make plays on the ball. If a fielder catches a ball on the fly, he is up. If the ball is on the ground, the fielder throws the ball toward the bat which is now sitting on the ground. If he hits the bat, he is up. Surprisingly, the kids love this game. The older kids mostly know how to hit fungos, so this part is generally handled by the younger kids. Once we know each kid can hit a fungo, we go to Helter-Skelter. Helter-Skelter is played with two teams with fielders placed at third, short, second and first. If we have enough players, then someone will be placed on the mound, and another behind the plate.

The hitter must hit the ball out of his hand. If he hits it foul, he's out, if he pops up and its caught, he is out. If he swings and misses he's out. If the ball lands outside of the infield, i.e. on the outfield grass, it is an out.

After hitting the ball, the runner runs to first, and a play is made on him. If he reaches first safely, the next hitter's job is to move him over. Three outs and the teams change sides. Once again, the defense gets 10 seconds to get everyone off the field and a hitter in the box. The hitter can hit the ball anytime he gets into the box, provided all of his teammates are off the field. A ball through the infield is a single. A ball that goes through a fielder's legs is an automatic home run.

Because the teams are running helter-skelter to get the advantage over their opponents, most players play in the field with their helmets on, and when time is short, will often be in the field without their gloves, or will often leave their gloves on the field when at bat. The players help police their teammates. No one wants to lose. Lord help the player who does not hustle.

Runners get automatic singles when the ball gets by the infielders, but get to keep running if a ball is thrown away, or dropped by a fielder either on a throw or a muffed pop up.

Once again, hustle is at a premium.

It really is a great sight watching kids hustle all over the field.

Chapter 10

You Must Have A Plan (Even A Crappy Plan Is Better Than None At All)

As can be seen, we have a pretty strong philosophy that we try to follow. That becomes part of our "plan."

I believe that it is difficult to succeed in baseball without a plan, without an approach. What many people don't realize is that there are different approaches to the game. Regardless of your approach, you need to believe in it, practice it, and preach it.

I often tell our players that our approach is not the only approach, and our plan is not the only plan. But it is our plan, embrace it. Tailor it to your personnel, and your personality. I often use the example of John Wooden and his UCLA basketball teams. In 1964, UCLA had nobody over 6'5", so they rolled out a zone press and won the national championship.

They then signed a 7'2" center named Lou Alcindor and changed their style of play to make the most of his abilities. After winning three more championships, Lou graduated. Without the monster in the middle, Wooden changed his approach again, this time using a troika of power forwards (Rowe, Wicks and Patterson), and won multiple championships. When they graduated, he then turned back the clock and used Bill Walton to keep the championship mill going. After watching my son's college team play in the spring in California, his coach asked me what I thought. When I asked him what type of team he wanted, he looked at me with a jaundiced eye.

"What do you mean?" "I mean, what type of team do you want?" "One that wins" he said. "Yes, but what style?" I asked again. I then went on to explain using the John Wooden example. When I explained this to the coach he shunned me, walked away and never spoke to me again. Our plan is based on aggressiveness and I try to tailor it to our personnel.

Every coach I know wants his pitcher to throw a strike with his first pitch, and to get ahead in the count.

Since more than 80% of all first pitches are "get it over" fastballs, why not have your kids look for that pitch. If they have played enough one strike game, they are ready. We look for a first pitch fastball every time we are up. If we are wrong, the good Lord still gives us two more strikes.

We have the same philosophy at 2-0, and at 3-1. On my team, you do not get fooled by a 2-0 fastball. At every count we are "looking for a pitch to kill." I never tell a kid, "two strikes, protect." That is defensive. Instead I yell, "two strikes, look for a pitch to kill!"

Our plan, reinforced by the one strike game, the line game and our forms of bp, result in fearless, aggressive hitters, at every age. We try to diminish what I call two strike panic by embracing an aggressive approach. When we strike out, we generally go down swinging. We are aggressive on the bases as well. We believe that to be a necessary part of our "plan."

We also try to inculcate defense as part of our plan.

1.) If you are not moving somewhere you are screwing up. That means moving to a position to back up a throw, an error, or a dive.
2.) Always assume the person ahead of you is going to biff. That means, for example, the left fielder charges a grounder to short, thinking the shortstop will biff. The

right fielder charges to back up first thinking the short stop will throw the ball away. The center fielder actually charges on any pick off attempt at second.

3.) A play is never over until its over. Never take it for granted that a play is concluded. We always want our hitters to have a plan. Sometimes that plan will change. One game our lead off JV hitter went to a full count to start a game. Five pitches, all fastballs. The sixth pitch was a curve ball that he took for strike three. The next hitter also worked the count, and drew five fastballs to get to 3-2. If he paid any attention at all, he should have known he was going to see a curve ball, just like our first hitter. Everyone in the park knew the curve was coming except the hitter who took it for strike three. Yet he was surprised when the pitcher struck him out on a 3-2 curve!

I can't tell you how many guys are fooled by 2-0 fastballs. Not only do you need a plan, you need to focus on what's happening around you. Kids that understand this are few and far between.

One day our Sun Belt College group was playing in a tournament in Warren Ball Park in Bisbee, Arizona, a cavernous ball park that is said to be the oldest ball park in America. It truly is a scenic old park in a scenic mountain town. The field is large, and bleachers are set up in right field for when the stadium is used for local high school football. As usual, we were short players, so one of the players, Chris, brought his junior in high school brother to play with us. The brother was facing a pitcher who had pitched in the D-3 World Series. After working the count to 3-2, the pitcher threw a wicked curve ball. Strike three! As he took off his batting gloves to get ready to get back on the field he looked at me and told me the next time he was up he was going to hit that curve ball 500 feet. I admired his confidence.

The next time he was up he let five pitches go by, looking totally disinterested. He made no effort to swing and seemed like he wanted to be anywhere but in the batters box against this monster college pitcher. He looked to the bench, and I swear he winked at me. He knew what was coming, exactly what was coming, and he was ready for it. The pitcher knew the kid couldn't hit his curve, so here it came. And there it went. It was hit so hard, it went over the bleachers. Yes, this kid had a plan. For most of this year that youngster, Alex Verdugo, has been one of the leading hitters in the National League for the Dodgers.

Chapter 11

How We Practice

We usually have a pretty simple but organized and flexible format for practice, varying based on the age, skill level, mistakes made during games, and ability of the team.

The first part of warmups includes a lap, stretches, pliometrics (high knees, butt kickers, Kariokie, bounding, and short quick steps, always starting with a cross over step) and then throwing, which always includes long toss. Guys who pitch spend at least 1/3 of their time throwing with their change up grip. We love competition, so we then bring the players close together and play a game of quick hands and quick feet. Two guys per team. Generally around 30 throws (up and back is one), sometimes more, as they progress. If a ball hits the ground for any reason, they go back to zero. The first team to the prescribed number of throws without a drop wins. Everyone else runs. The game is over when one team wins for the second time. We then slide just about every day. Our next phase of practice will be team specific. Usually something new we want to expose everyone to, or something we did not do well at our last game. We'll then break down into a number of groups. Except for hitting, we don't use stations as such. For the first round of what I call breakdowns, I may have two catchers work on throw downs (I usually have our catchers at home and second during throwing warmups so they are totally used to throwing from home to second), or blocking. I may have 2 third basemen (sometimes only one) working on making throws on the run, and a couple of shortstop middle infielders drilling on moving their feet (i.e coming around the ball, fielding balls on the move, etc).

At the same time, we'll have a couple of outfielders working on various aspects of outfield work.

After a prescribed period, we will then have another rotation with different drills with players placed in groups and given tasks based on their needs. So while each rotation has the kids doing something different, it is not quite like having stations. For us stations work best for hitting groups.

By now, we have used up about 1 ½ hours of practice time. Sometimes more, sometimes less. We've been all business, so far, working hard. Believe me, when you keep small groups of 3 or less, you can get an amazing series of repetitions done. We try never to have everybody at short, for example, and hit ground balls. We may have 3 groups of 3 or less doing that. Believe me, the kids get really tired. There is absolutely no time for them to fool around, because no sooner do they get back in their position than they are required to perform some other baseball related action. Then we may do infield/outfield.

Once that is done, it is play time. Truly the reason most kids come to practice. I can't tell you how many times the kids have asked to play more, even though their parents or rides have come to get them. I tell folks, if you need your kid, just take him. For the older kids, if they need to go, then just go. We'll just adjust the teams.

On Saturday mornings I like to start practice early. I then often allow the kids to play our games as long as they (and even their parents) are willing.

Kids love this part of practice so much, that rarely, before high school, did we practice with just our team alone.

Kids from other teams and of other ages (often including older and younger brothers-and in some cases sisters) come to our practices. The only rule for them is that they play by the same rules as everyone else and participate just like our "regular" team members do.

That has gotten me in trouble with other coaches, for "stealing" their players and league officials who, for some reason, don't think it is seemly for kids not on our team to practice with us.

Some coaches have simply refused to allow their kids to attend our practices. Sometimes our own parents will object because "we shouldn't be teaching other kids to play, that is the job of their "real" coach.

That has simply never been my philosophy.

One year in Legion we had a youngster play in a couple of early season tournaments with us. Because our school enrollment would be out of wack if he played for us, I found him a spot on another team.

When we played that other team, Joe got the game winning RBI. Some folks on our side were furious. What I did was treason. Definitely an impeachable offense. Sorry, I just didn't feel that way. I was proud of Joe for delivering in the clutch, and not so proud of our pitcher who grooved one for Joe.

What made folks even more upset was while we were playing a Legion game in a four field complex I received a call from Mark, the college coach at Upper Iowa wanting to speak to Joe so he could offer him a college scholarship. I had to round up Joe who was playing on anther team in another game on an adjacent field.

He was offered right in the middle of the game. When confronted by some irate folks, I told them that if they were unhappy, they could play elsewhere and may beat us in the 9th, just like Joe did. I also told them that the game is for the kids, and that I was proud that I could help another kid.

Joe got a spot with Upper Iowa University, played there for four years and earned his degree.

Isn't that the kind of thing we are supposed to do? One year we took our team to a Legion tournament at the Field of Dreams in Iowa.

It took awhile to dawn on the players that we were really at the Field of Dreams until one of the players in surprise yelled

"That's the road, that's the road." All of a sudden it was real to them. Twenty three hours of driving, and here we were!

After we arrived at the field we changed into our spikes ready to take the field. Suddenly a woman came running out of the house (yes the same house that's in the movie) next to the field. "Get off my field in those spikes!" she yelled. "We spent hours this morning getting the field ready!"

We were startled. Come on!! Nobody owns the Field of Dreams! Actually the Lansing family did own it, or about half of it. The other half was owned by another group called Left and Center Field of Dreams (definitely no love lost between the two groups).

We did Mrs. Lansing's bidding, and took off our spikes before entering the field. She turned out to be a very wonderful and gracious woman.

One of my players was sitting alone on the side of the field. I went to check and see if something was wrong. He was on the telephone to his father who was stationed in Korea. I over heard him say: "Dad, you'll never guess where we are."

Another player told me it wasn't real, and if guys came out of the corn field, he would "pass out.". My wife and I got to play catch at the Field of Dreams. Yes, it's a magical place.

Unbeknownst to the players, I had arranged for the "Ghost Players" most of whom were in the Field of Dreams movie to surprise our guys by appearing magically out of the cornfield. Needless to say, we made memories that day.

One of the "Ghosts" was the Upper Iowa coach, Coach Danker. Through the years, Coach Danker recruited quite a number of our players. A couple of months ago I had dinner with the Coach and a host of Upper Iowa Tucson area alums. A good time was had by all.

The Ghost players came out of the field, but because they only owned half of the field, they could not come to the home plate area due to their territorial dispute with the Lansing family.

While we were in Iowa, every player on our squad received multiple offers.

Our first game in that tournament was played on an island in the Mississippi. Before coming to Iowa I emailed 20 or more college coaches that we were coming. When we arrived at Petrakis Field, I could not believe my eyes when about 20 college coaches met us there. They love Western kids who get to play all year round.

We also had a chance to hit in the cages at Clarke College. While doing so, my least accomplished player took his turn in the cage.

"Wow, nice swing" said the coach. I agreed.

"Would he travel?" he asked

"Without hesitation."

"Why, would you take him?" "In a New York second."

When the player came out of the cage the Coach took him aside and signed him on the spot. He spent four years at Clarke.

I would not have missed this experience for all the all stars in the world.

We have been very lucky being able to find college homes for our players.

Chapter 12

You Can't Play Baseball
With A Tight Rear End

Everything comes down to this fact. Baseball is a game and needs to be played. It isn't work. No one can be successful in this, the hardest of all games, playing with a tight sphincter. If you can't enjoy it, why do it?

Sometimes people have accused us of being too loose, but most of the time it has held us in good stead. I remember one time we had a powerhouse club, and were playing in the 58 team wooden bat, High Desert Classic in Albuquerque. It was the final day, and as usual we had but 10 players. The day was rainy, and games all over the valley were either seriously delayed, or moved to different fields. To win the tournament we'd need to win three games that Sunday. Our first game was against a monster team, the East L. A. Dodgers. They were a big, talented, ugly, trash talking crew. They let us know that they turned up at the field poised to end our misery in short order. They definitely looked mean enough to do it.

Their pitcher threw gas, a "heavy" ball (especially devastating on a cold day), and almost every pitch was on the inside, or off the inside of the plate, breaking numerous of our wood bats.

We were down two runs in the bottom of the last inning. When our guys came off the field I was exhorting them to show some energy and emotion both of which seemed to be lacking the whole game. As I was ranting, Bryan, our third baseman, (whose Dad umpired a number of our games this past summer) put his arm around my shoulders and said: "Coach, calm down, this is KFC and what we do is win tournaments. Chill. That's what we do."

Sure enough, four batters later the game was over, we won, and went on to win the tournament.

When we beat the great Taylorsville, Utah, team in the American Legion West Regional in 2000, the kids never doubted for an instant what would happen. As the Taylorsville 9 got more and more frustrated our guys got looser and looser. It wasn't even a game.

When one of my grand kids was a 12 year old, we had an especially good, but very small team. Everyone towered over us. But, boy could we run. Could we ever run. We took an undefeated team into a neighboring Little League district. When we arrived, it was clear that physically we were over matched. The pitcher, a 6'3" kid we called "the Mutant" had a 70 plus fastball (that's hard and demanding at the Little League distance of 45 feet, and not a little scary, make that a lot scary). He terrorized our league, and seemingly hit a home run every time he was up against one of our teams. He was the biggest, and meanest guy in the league.

In our first game with him pitching, we did not even touch the ball in the first three innings. Nine up and nine down. Nine ks, no foul balls even. We ended up with one hit and one walk for the game. Did that deter our kids? Not a bit. The kids decided that we would never lose to the mutant again, and had us throwing batting practice from very close, and very hard. They would be ready for him the next time. And they were.

We devised a game plan the next time we met that included pitching him inside with curves, and the harder he hit the ball foul, the slower our next pitch would be. We wanted to frustrate him, and frustrate him we did. Every pitch seemed slower than the last. As he got frustrated, his team followed his lead. Soon their heads were drooping. If their big guy couldn't hit, what chance did they have? On the other hand, we were going after his first pitch fastball at every at bat. Soon, as often happens, he started complaining of arm trouble. Our kids were loose, and never lost to the mutant again.

Those little runts didn't know that they were over matched. And that's how we played.

Chapter 13

Muscle Memory

Sometimes we all think we are great coaches, and contain all of the world's baseball wisdom. But when we look more closely, perhaps not. We're just too used to letting things slide.

Nine years ago I coached a boy in 9-10 Little League All-stars. Call him Billy for the purpose of this book.

Billy was a terrific young athlete, with far above average tools. Yet, when he got in the batters box his feet moved constantly, as if he were dancing. We called it the Billy dance. We did our best to break him of the habit over the approximately one and a half weeks that he was with us.

Fast forward nine years.

I was helping to coach an American Legion team during the summer of 2015. One of the players who joined us for the summer was the same boy, Billy, now 9 years older, and the recipient of a scholarship to play at an area junior college.

I had not recognized him until I saw a player enter the batter's box, and as the pitch was on its way, he did the Billy dance, just as he had done nine years earlier. Having gone from t-ball through high school ball a number of times, I have, unfortunately, seen the same scene repeated again and again, all over town. The defects learned early continue on.

Why didn't I do a better job when I had him? Instead I fell back on the old "I only had him for a couple of weeks, so what was I supposed to do?" The typical baseball coach lament.

The trouble is, when that pattern repeats itself, is it the kid's fault, or ours?

Why does the kid who took the huge uppercut to hit t-ball home runs, continue to swing the same way years later? Why does the chubby kid who opens his shoulders in minors continue to fly open in Pony and beyond?

How many hundreds, and thousands of unfortunate kids ended up leaving the game because they could never transition their mechanics to a more mature game? Purely because we are simply not doing a good job teaching.

Yes, I know, we alibi for ourselves by claiming that it is extremely difficult to change techniques ingrained over time. Why, I asked myself, do we see so many Little League superstars who don't make the grade later on? Sure, some don't mature, some run in place while other kids are catching up to them. Does it have to be this way?

I don't think so.

We need to drastically change how these kids do things, how we teach and how they learn.

We actually have the ability to do so.

I had the opportunity to help coach pitchers at a local high school. I decided that it was necessary to make fundamental changes in the way pitchers practice and do their bullpen work.

First, I rejected the model used by so many to have their pitchers do lengthy bull pen sessions a couple of times per week. Instead, I had our pitchers throw every day, using the Atlanta Braves approach. The key was to have them throw everyday, but to stop, not when they got tired, but when they felt they were about to start tiring. The goal was to have their arms stronger at season's end than at the beginning.

Secondly, we changed how they did their "pens." It made no sense to me to have a kid throw a couple of pitches outside, a couple inside, a couple of curves, a couple of changes and then repeat that routine. Instead, we decided to maximize muscle memory. Does a player gain muscle memory by throwing to different parts of the plate during practice?

I thought not. So I went to this model. I changed how I taught. Each pitcher in the program threw every day. Each pitcher was required to throw ten straight pitches low and away to a right handed hitter if they were right handed, and ten straight pitches low and away to a lefty batter if they were left handed. If unsuccessful, they had to keep at it until they got their ten in a row.

The catcher set up on the outside part of the plate with a four inch piece of black leather set two inches on home plate, and two inches off the plate. The pitcher had to hit the black ten straight times to end that part of the exercise. Any pitch that missed meant starting back at zero. Almost universally the kids had trouble completing the drill for the first week or so of practice.

We also met with resistence, since this was not how coaches around town approached pitching. We stuck with our approach, and when the pitchers began to hit their spots regularly and continually, the attitude changed, as did their ability to control the strike zone. Our inexperienced team went way farther in the Arizona State Tournament than anyone envisioned.

At some point in every game most pitchers seem to lose their rhythm and wonder what they are doing on the mound. These exercises help the pitcher keep his equilibrium and continue to make good pitches. Muscle memory makes for good muscle discipline.

After hitting the outside, they moved on to phase two, 10 straight up and in. The four inch piece of leather was moved adjacent to home plate on the inside. We did this because if you miss an inside pitch over the plate, it will end up being for extra bases. When throwing outside, getting the outside two inches plus two inches off the plate would not generally lead to as much damage. Plus, with umpires setting up on the inside shoulder of the catcher, balls two inches off the plate appear to be strikes.

Once successful, they could then begin work on their off speed pitches, as long as they worked their spots.

This approach has proven to be successful at every age. The kids arms remained strong, and they walked very few batters.

The line game and the one strike game were parts of the same philosophy. Muscle memory and brain memory. Do things right all the time, and soon it translates into how you play the game. For example, after a season of playing the line game, hitting the ball up the middle becomes routine. After a while the ball is hit up the middle with excruciating regularity.

During one Little League game we had 18 base hits up the middle. The other coach thought we were the luckiest team in America.

"You guys are so lucky, everything you hit had eyes and went up the middle." When I told him with a smile that it must be the coaching, he scoffed.

They become so used to having only one chance to hit a strike that two strike panic virtually disappears. They have been trained to handle the pressure. We have created literally hundreds of two strike hitters.

One year when Rusty made the Southern Arizona All Region team, the all region pitcher was asked about pitching to him. His answer: "I hated pitching to him. Everybody could get two strikes on him, but once he had two strikes, you just couldn't get him out," as his over .500 average showed.

Over the years I have become quite self satisfied with how our kids learned from these silly little games, and from our muscle and brain training games.

What we were doing was good, but not good enough.

Coaching is not easy. Solutions and magic don't materialize out of thin air. Instead of throwing our hands up and deciding that if we practiced hard on our technique, and if they couldn't learn it, well, "that's life." After all, not everyone is meant to be a super baseball player. Not everyone can play high school and later college ball.

I decided that I was deluding myself, and "copping" out. While that was partially true, it was no excuse. We could, and should do better.

After weeks of frustration with a pretty sorry team (and after getting creamed by the team that had all of the "better" players), I decided to change my method, and experimented with this less than average group of nine year olds who just didn't seem to catch on to the idea of throwing and catching.

I had all of the parents on the field, and explained to them that I wanted their kids to go through a prescribed "shadow" throwing motion at least 25 times per night, every night, before bed, and that I would hold them responsible if they didn't follow through with their kids.

I also gave each kid a tennis ball and told the parents they were to throw the tennis balls slowly to their kids who had to catch 25 in a row in their glove hand every night before bed time.

Even I was surprised how the team progressed mightily. When the final game of the season was upon us, we were playing the "stud" team.

This time the shoe was on the other foot, and we were the murderers, and they were the murdered. Our kids were asking in the dugout, "Coach, we thought they were good?" I told them they were good, but we worked harder, and were now better.

I soon realized, you simply can't get enough repetitions during practice to really affect ingrained patterns. You have to be innovative and find ways to have them repeat the motions you need hundreds, or even thousands of times (instead of the dozen or so times you can do so at a practice).

To get rid of the old and bring on the new, you must act decisively. When you do it right, even the resistant kids and parents seem to catch on. The truth is, it is easier to influence the kids than the parents. After all, this was not how they remembered it from when they were "Little League heros."

One year, after watching our pitchers stand straight up during their delivery, and not moving straight to home plate, often falling off the mound, I had enough.

I had to drastically change what we were doing and the way we were doing it. I had all of our pitchers in a line, and showed them how I wanted them to stand, extend their stride, step straight, and throw the ball overhand, ending with their chests over their front knee, and their arms extended through the pitch. That is all we did during the entire practice. Boy, did the parents squeal. They knew their Coach was crazy. They had to do the motion three hundred or more times.

If that was not bad enough, we repeated the exercise again the very next day. They had to do the same thing the entire week. When we finally let them actually throw, they were unbelievably better finishing with their bodies, and getting and keeping the ball down. It was all in the muscle memory. We made them do this (and I know many of them hated me and the drill) until the old patterns were broken.

Recently, I had similar issues with a 12-13 year old group that I was coaching. We re-instituted the same program with the pitchers. Did it work? You bet it did. Does that mean we made Nolan Ryan's out of everybody? No, of course not. But they sure were better.

Often in order to get kids on board I would do what I could to dream up new solutions. For example, one day I took one of our players aside. When hitting, he would drop his hands and had a terrible upswing. He let practically every ball get in on his hands, and it would either be popped up or missed (the latter being the most likely event).

I took the bat from him and took he and his parents aside and told them that I would fix his swing if it took me the entire season. I loaned him my Oscar Miller Swing Rite T. It has holes for tees to be placed in it. One tee was placed behind the other.

The back Tee was higher than the front one. Balls were placed on both tees. There was simply no way he could upswing and only hit the front tee. I made him spend the entire practice working hitting only the front ball. He took the tee home and continued to work.

We estimate he took at least one thousand good swings off the Swing Rite.

Now he was ready. In his first game he went three for three, not an upswing in the bunch. We were very proud.

The name of the game is muscle memory. Use it to your best advantage.

Chapter 14

Respect The Baseball Gods

There are many unwritten rules of baseball, violation of which I find totally offensive, and which regularly get punished by the baseball gods. Sometimes the baseball gods are cruel. Believe me!! I have seen it many times in my life.

When Rusty was 11 and 12, we had a team we were sure would take our kids to the world series. Then the unthinkable happened. Our star lefty pitcher broke his leg. We finished in the top three out of the 24 leagues in Tucson. Our kids knew, had Rick not broken his leg, we were sure to have made it to Williamsport.

Rick (who later became the head of the FC Tucson soccer club) was back the next year, bigger and better than ever. Between the end of the regular Little League season and the start of All Stars, he once again was playing soccer, and for the second straight season (no, that's not possible), he broke his leg. Once again we came up one pitcher, and one win short. Yes, the fates can be cruel.

As my co-coach Vic and I were sitting around bemoaning our fate before our kids started Junior League on the "big field." We truly felt sorry for ourselves. All our visions of success were dashed. There went our big chance.

While we were sitting at Palo Verde Park (the TV home of Johnny Bench and the Baseball Bunch), a shadow came over us. As we looked up, as the Lord is my witness, there he stood, Matt, a new kid who just moved into our Little League boundaries, all left handed 6'3" of him. Were we dreaming or what? Could this be happening?

It could and did. Matt became an integral part of our team for years, and helped us win at least four City Championships.

At other times, as I noted, the baseball overseers could be less benign.

One of those times came in a 12 year old Little League fall baseball season in Tucson. My wife and I were a spectators.

One of our grandkids played on a team coached by a golf pro. You'd think a golfer would appreciate the rules of etiquette governing his sport. Unfortunately this person did not.

He refused to teach his players the most rudimentary and important rules of baseball deportment, like "respecting the lines," not walking across the infield during inning changes, and calling time out before entering the field of play. This baseball sinner was punished for these continued transgressions many times. Our grandson was on a tremendous streak, with ten straight hits, reaching base thirteen times in a row. After getting his tenth hit, he almost hopped out to the outfield just barely missing the third base line (whew!!!). On the way back at the end of the inning, without paying attention and without respecting the laws of baseball, he stepped right on the foul line.

"Oh, no!!" I exclaimed in a stage whisper as Brandon was getting ready to lead off the inning. I muttered "he just stepped right on the line. His hit streak is over!." My wife, a lawyer, and an avid fan, is sadly untutored in "baseball law." She dared to scoff at me.

"Superstition" she said, "silly superstition."

"Just watch" I said, "Just watch. I just hope he doesn't get hurt."

Scoffed again, she did. She just knew the man she married was crazy and had flipped his lid.

Well, Brandon got up, and three pitches later walked dejectedly back to the dugout a strikeout victim. A punishment for violating sacred tradition. My worries were validated.

But that didn't end this team's tempting fate and angering the baseball gods. In the top of the 6th and last inning, Brandon's team went ahead 9-2, when the unbelievable and unimaginable happened!

The coach (a phrase I use advisedly) unforgivably stepped on the third base line. Then, not happy with angering the baseball gods, walked across the infield-(impeding players from the other team going on the field and throwing warm up pitches), and then compounded the issue by purposefully stepping full flush on the first base line.

"OMG" I muttered (showing my savvy-ness in modern text language). "Did you see that!. He defiled the third base line, walked across the infield, and then defiled the first base line. No good will come of this, I tell you, no good will come of this."

Once again my dear wife scoffed. "Will you stop it already." (She was a little exasperated by then with me)

"I can't watch" I told her. "I just can't watch."

Three pitchers later, and 6 line "steppings later," the score was 9-7 with the bases loaded. Sure enough, a kid who had struck out twice before came up, and tied the score. It was now 9-9. The coach, who typically came out of the dugout and entered the field without calling time, did his usual. This time, when he did, the runner on third was ready for him, and scored the winning run.

And, you know what this coach did! He screamed at the home plate umpire who had taken off his mask during the play. "You took off your mask" he screamed. "Time was out." Sorry Dude, time was not out, because you didn't ask for it.

When he finally went back to the dugout after costing his kids the game, he didn't even let his kids shake hands with the opposing team. This activated my wife who ran screaming to the dugout. "No," she yelled. "No, no, no!!"

She ran up, confronted the coach and told him to get his players back out on the field to shake hands. She was livid. An assistant coach finally ordered the kids back out on the field. They finally went to shake hands with the other team, now congregating with their coach in left field.

Very bad things happen when you are ignorant of the basic laws of baseball, or purposely flaunt them. Very bad things. We can't be responsible for such things Often times the results are more subtle. In the year 2000, the 75th year of Legion Baseball, after our team won the first of four straight double headers needed to qualify or post season play, all but one of the players decided that we shouldn't wash the good luck out of our uniforms. The one player who refused "couldn't hit anyway" and really was "only a pitcher" so our guys thought they could overcome his heresy. As luck would have it, we ran up an impressive winning streak getting us to the state finals. To say our team was "rank" would be the understatement of the year. I had a major problem. How could we keep the gods of baseball happy without washing the luck out of our uniforms? I had a day off to solve the problem while we waited to see which team would play us for the championship. Legion (which pays for everything in State and National competition-including paying meal money to the kids) had housed us at a beautiful resort in the Phoenix area with a huge Olympic sized swimming pool.

An idea was formed. I called a team meeting with full uniforms (less shoes) and marched everyone out to the pool (to the astonishment of the hundreds of resort guests keeping themselves cool and lubricated). "Gentlemen, the ritual bath is the foundation of most of the world's sacred religions. It's called a 'mikvah' in the Jewish religion. Hindus take their ritual baths in the Ganges. And Christians go through baptism. Now, to appease the baseball gods and to assure ourselves of victory tomorrow, it is our time to go through the baseball ritual bath." On the count of three, our team leapt into the pool (uniforms and all, less spikes) amid gasps from the pool side vacationers. A bathtub ring of epic proportions surrounded the pool as dirt oozed from their uniforms. A crowd gathered to watch this display. One of the groups watching was our fierce rivals from Tucson High School. Yes, they loudly scoffed.

I warned them, "...you dare scoff the baseball gods. And for that, you will be punished. You, though heavily favored, will lose tonight. We won't get to face you for the championship."

And lose they did. And win we did.

Yes, offend the baseball gods at your own risk!

Chapter 15

Why Do Kids Seem To Play Better And Harder For You?

Players play their hardest when they want to play, not because you tell them to play hard. They play hard when they care for the team, don't like the opponents, care for their teammates, and even care for the coach.

Kids like success and to be part of something "great." Kids play great when they expect to win.

Kids play great when they want to win.

Kids play great when they have the freedom to "play" the game.

Isn't it part of a coaches job to get the most out of his players?

We tell our kids, if you can run, run. If you can run, don't waste it by becoming a statue at first. Run, something good will happen.

And yes, as noted earlier in the imaginary letter referred to in the introduction, I had a second base/shortstop player (and later a first team all American second baseman at the University of New Mexico) who played for our Legion team from the time he was 13 until he aged out. He did indeed steal on practically every first pitch.

People knew it was coming, and the pressure on the catcher was great to stop him. They were mostly unsuccessful. Pitchers would get distracted. Throw after throw went to first, usually leading to an errant throw by the catcher.

We tell our players: "If you can hit, hit. If you can field, field. If you are an outgoing person, then be outgoing. If you are tough, be tough. Just be who you are."

It's amazing how much you can get from a kid when you just let him be who he is.

We try to take a simple approach to our players. We have to assess who can play, and what will work.

"Coach Yoda and friend, May 4, 2018. It is not magic or the force, it comes down to great coaching."

A few examples.

One day a left-handed kid from one of our schools showed up with his Dad. The kid wasn't physically imposing (about my size), and seemingly quite shy. His Dad asked if we had a spot for him. I went to the bullpen and watched him throw.

Nothing great, but he certainly had some innings in his arm. I made one simple change. Before his right foot landed giving him a firm base, his shoulders and arm began moving forward. What I did was have him stay back, land his front foot first, and then throw over his front leg. Voila, he added an easy five mph to his pitches.

Next we changed his arm circle. Instead of putting pressure on his shoulder, we had him throw as if he were conducting an orchestra, modeling his delivery more like a softball pitcher with a more circular motion. Voila, another 5 mph.

He still didn't throw gas, but he was now near 80.

He became a serviceable pitcher for us, and began getting regular mound time at his high school.

The next season (after his senior year) he came out to play with us again. I asked him to show me his change up. He didn't have one. Four years at the high school and he had no change!!!

So we stood near the storage wall of the home dugout, and started bouncing a ball off the wall using a circle change grip. Voila, again. After about three pitches he had a change up. A devastating change. But still, he had no place to play in college. He didn't throw hard enough to attract much attention.

With his new found change he quickly became an ace for us. He'd get ahead with his fastball, and then start throwing his curve and change at people.

He was tremendously effective. When in Albuquerque for the High Desert Classic tournament, I brought him in to pitch just as the head coach for Colorado State walked in the park. He faced nine batters, struck out nine batters, and gained the attention of the CSU coach, and a scholarship as well.

I wish I could say he kicked butt in Colorado, but things didn't work out for him, so he transferred to Armstrong-Atlantic where he led the entire nation in victories. Another overlooked guy getting a chance to pitch.

Overlooking kids seems almost to be a national disease.

One year a tall skinny kid (Joey) was interested in playing for us. The kid played at a local Catholic school, and was not given many innings. The instant I saw him, I knew he could pitch. And pitch he did. Just a few tweaks here and there and encouragement was all that was needed.

One season he pitched every tough game we played, and was truly awesome. Before he was through he had the second most wins in the history of our Legion program. He pitched junior college and four year college ball, and today is the head coach for a junior college in Iowa.

When we needed a big win against a powerhouse Albuquerque Baseball Academy team one year (they threw three guys throwing 92, 94 and 97 at us), he got it for us.

When we faced elimination in the West Regional tournament and needed a win to stay alive, he got it for us. When we needed a win in the Arizona State Championships, he got it for us. When we needed someone to get Bryce Harper out, it was Joey.

It's job of the coach to help these players chase their dreams. That's what we always tried to do.

One year, Joey was beating our biggest rival in the Arizona State tournament. When he reached his pitch limit (it was an artificial limit set by me-this was before "pitch" counting came into vogue) we were ahead by eight. I brought in my number two who suddenly collapsed. He had been great all year long, until this game.

The other team came from behind, scored 9 runs, and we lost a sure victory. You can bet folks were angry. Why did I take out my starter when he had them totally off balance and on the ropes!! Why did I bring in this kid!!!. Yes, that clinched, the Coach really was an idiot.

But, sometimes you simply have to stick by your guns and philosophy, regardless of how it makes you look. I simply wasn't going to allow Joey too many pitches.

Our number two became an excellent college closer, and I felt he could do the job, just as he had done all season. I simply wasn't going to risk Joey's arm by leaving him in.

As luck would have it, the loss didn't hurt us too badly, and we made it back to the championship game against our rivals, winner take all.

The coaches from the other team were scared to death that we would be starting Joey in the championship game.

I assured them I wasn't going to pitch Joey, because I felt he needed more than one day of rest. They even went so far as to lobby Joey's parents not to let me pitch their kid again, because they didn't want to harm his future as a pitcher.

I kept telling them I was going to pitch Matt. "Who is he?", they asked. "Another guy from the Catholic school." These guys were in the same conference as the Catholic school, and still didn't know who Matt was.

They were unrelenting, because they knew that I would pitch Joey against them, despite everything I said. They knew they could not hit Joey. They never had.

So who was Matt? Matt was a strong armed guy who didn't get to pitch much for his high school because he had control issues.

We changed some of his mechanics, and brought him along slowly during our Legion season. He pitched an inning here, and inning there, and more innings in tournaments out of town. By the time of the State Championship, we were confident he could do the job.

And do the job he did. 18 K's, and one scratch hit later we were State Champions, and Matt was the winning pitcher. Every time I would walk to the 3rd base coaching box the other team coaches kept asking me: "Who is this guy?"

"Just like I told you, Matt."

Our shortstop on that team was small. Nobody took him seriously because of his size. I thought he was terrific, and as good as any of the other seven or eight drafted shortstops we've had. It took some effort, but Chris ended up at Trinity College in San Antonio, and after his college career, he was signed by the Cardinals.

His brother was a lightly regarded player who played left field for us. They hit back to back home runs in the championship game pitched by Matt.

Overall, a very satisfactory season.

When kids have fun, enjoy what they are doing, and can't wait to play, they do extraordinary things.

I recruited a lefty, Mike, a pitcher from a local high school. He was so successful that he was drafted by the Indians after his senior year. He was invited to a series of post season all star games involving the best players Arizona had to offer.

During one of those games, something horrible happened. While delivering a pitch, he suddenly felt a terrible pain in his shoulder. He came out of the game immediately. From the height of excitement to the depths of despair. Surgery was inevitable.

If his promising career weren't over, it sure would be delayed. No Legion Baseball that summer for him. Rehab wasn't enough. Surgery was the only viable alternative. That would take at least a full year away from him. So much promise halted by injury. Such misfortune would crush most players.

When we began preparing for the next summer season, we brought our players together for a practice (something our Legion teams rarely did since we were playing 50 or more games per summer in about 60 days). Mike showed up.

I asked him what he was doing there. He told me he wanted to play Legion with us during the summer. I told him no, he couldn't play. He was not ready to pitch, and his j c coach would string me up if I let him play.

He said watch. He went out to centerfield and had us hit him a fungo. That's what we did. He caught the ball in medium center field and threw it on a line to second base right handed. "See," he said, "I've been practicing all winter."

Once we picked our jaws off the ground, we decided to let him play. And play he did. He told me he wasn't interested in pitching (though during a get together he struck out our All-American second baseman right handed).

When he started in center we were 17-3, and while not known as a hitter, he even hit the daylights out of the ball all summer. His incandescent personality made him one of the best leaders we've ever had. His indomitable determination was an inspiration to all.

Today he is an age group coach for a local club team. We even played his team with our recent 13 U team.

The Most Amazing KFC Finish Ever

One year we were playing in our local American Legion tournament, playing for the right to advance to State competition. We were on the edge of elimination. A loss, and we would be eliminated.

But, as luck would have it, we were playing one of our fiercest rivals. They just didn't like me, or our team. They were always talented but had a record of futility against us.

This particular year they were loaded. They had two University of Arizona pitchers, one a mean submariner, the other a guy who threw in the 90's. They were big, experienced, confident and mean.

Before the game, the rains came. I visited the fields which were underwater, and knew we would not be playing that night. A short while later, I was called by the league commissioner who told me our game was to be postponed. I called our players to let them know.

A Tucson monsoon does not usually cover our entire valley, and sometimes moves erratically so that a game will be rained out a short distance from another field that could be as dry as a bone. Sometimes the rain will hit, and leave quickly enough that the field can be made ready again for play.

About two hours after canceling our game, I received a call from the Commissioner, "be ready to go by 7:30 PM at Arthur Pack," a field about 45 minutes away from my home clear on the north side of town.

The team we were playing was from the area of the field. So I did a mad scramble. I called and texted everyone I could reach.

My scheduled starting pitcher (a future D-1 player at Manhattan and the son of a major leaguer), my shortstop, and my outfield could not be reached.

When they were told the game was cancelled, they all decided to go to the movies together. Sometimes having the players enjoy each other's company has its drawbacks. I tinkered with the idea of calling all the theaters in town and announcing an emergency. Coolers heads kept me from doing so.

When 7:25 came, we had only 8 players, and would surely forfeit (despite my constant complaints about unfairness). As the clock struck 7:30, our ninth player showed up. Just in the nick of time. Five minutes later and we would have been out of the tournament, our season over. Not fair, not fair at all. But, as I told our players that night, "life is not always fair. Deal with it. Who cares who is not here, lets be happy with who is here!!!"

Our starter was Joey, early in his tenure with us. He was used sparingly by his high school. Their starter was the fearsome submariner and University of Arizona pitcher.

We were missing a couple of our best hitters, pitchers and players.

But like always, we came to play.

The first inning started out rocky. A home run and a ground rule double put us behind in the very first inning.

But we clawed back, until we got into the late innings. We were down 4-1, then 5-2, but were running out of outs. In the 8th, we got runners on, and Jamie doubled for us. 5-3.

A pick off attempt at second on the still wet ground resulted in Jamie catching a spike and breaking his leg. His yell as he was hurt resounded throughout the park. We all ran out to him.

He was in total agony, rolling around on the ground. Under Legion Rules, a team can not play with fewer than nine players, regardless of the reason. If he could not play, we would forfeit.

After everything we had been through, it was certain that we would have to forfeit. We were left with no other choice. The game and our season were over.

But Jamie decided otherwise. As he was screaming in pain, he began to yell, "we are not going to forfeit this game! We are not going to forfeit this game!" Over and over he yelled.

We got him on his feet, and he demanded to stay in the game. He would not let us take him off the field. He stayed on base (literally on the base), in pain the entire time.

We loaded the bases, and could not score. We put Jamie on first base, and made alternate plans if they decided to try and bunt on us. Joey got tough, and somehow we got out of the inning without giving up a run.

But, we were down to our last three outs. In the top of the 9th, we got a couple of runners on and with two outs, we were still down 5-4, with Jamie being helped by teammates to the batter's box. The game was on the line. This was it. And, to make matters worse, they brought in Ricky (Rick later coached with me), their 90 plus thrower to get the last out and finish the game.

Things looked very bad for us.

As the new pitcher warmed up, I stood with Jamie who was still in great pain. He leaned on my shoulders as we watched the pitcher. I didn't know how he could hit the ball, let alone get to first base. I was pretty sure our season was about to come to an end.

"Remember Kirk Gibson?" I asked Jamie.

"They are bringing this kid in, just for you. He's going to throw you fastballs, so concentrate on just using your hands."

Pitch one, 89, strike one. Pitch two, 91 (and it looked even faster), strike two.

Third pitch 92, right down the middle. Jamie swung and hit a long fly ball to left center gap, that one hopped the fence. With the crack of the bat, Jamie began hopping on one leg to first base, the lead run scored, and Jamie, unbelievably, barely made it to first, but he made it. Luckily we were playing on a pretty large field, though the ball would have been out in most of Tucson's fields.

The team and fans were going crazy. But I didn't call time out. As they yelled at one another, I created a diversion going into hysterics yelling. From across he field near the first base dugout I really got on our runner on third for not scoring.

Everyone was screaming as Jamie neared first. While attention was split between Jamie and me, the runner, Tanner, jogged home with an insurance run.

The coach from the other team almost had apoplexy as we took an amazingly improbable two run lead.

Jamie stayed at first for the bottom of the ninth. Somehow we got out of the inning. Against all odds, we won. Without a doubt, the most fantastic KFC Legion finish in our history.

Chapter 16

Every Team, Indeed
Every Kid, Is Different

Coaching manuals continually warn coaches that all kids are different, but rarely mention that not only are the kids different, each team creates it own identity.

If a coach is not mindful of the differences between teams, he is missing an important ingredient in coaching. Not every coach is a fit for every team. That doesn't mean you should ever stop trying to be a fit.

I learned early on that one of our great teams (we went 62-4) didn't like to come to games early (and barely on time), hated to spend time talking (both pre and post game), but always were ready to answer the bell.

At first I gave them trouble about showing up late, and then decided because of the team's personality we would make a deal. If they wanted to show up late for games, they could do so, provided that when they showed, they had to be ready to play. They came ready, game in and game out. Their season record was 62-4.

They'd straggle in, show up just before game time and go out and annihilate people. I would be a nervous wreck waiting and hoping for a ninth player to show. They had this swagger when they took the field that anyone could see. They started off at the beginning of the season winning the Canyon State Games tournament.

Two weeks later they won the Prescott Invitational, two weeks after that they won the Tucson July 4 tournament, a week later won the 58 team High Desert Classic, two weeks after that won the Area A (Southern Arizona) Legion Tournament, and followed that up winning the Arizona State Championship by winning the final game against a favored team coached by a former Red Sox great and led by a Stanford starting pitcher by scoring more than 20 runs.

We were the underdogs. But, not in the minds of our guys. Even then, at the end of the game, we met in a group, me in the middle surrounded by our team towering over me, and they still didn't want to talk. A few high fives, and some "good games" and our celebration was over. I asked how they felt, and the answer was a simple one: "We get to play together for at least one more week." A monster group hug followed.

Any time I tried a motivational speech it didn't do any good. They had their style, and that's how they played.

On the other hand, recently I was helping out at a local high school, almost exclusively with the jv. Then one day the head coach asked me to accompany the varsity team out of town to Sierra Vista, Arizona, about 90 miles away. The first time we had played this team we got destroyed, and played terrible ball.

While the Coach was attending to head coach duties, I was in the outfield with the team. They told me they wanted to hear an inspirational speech. To hop them up for the game.

So that's what I did.

"Are you sure you want this? "Yes," they answered as a group.

"You sure, because when I do this I don't fool around." "Yes, do it."

"Well gentlemen," I said, "Here goes."

"I saw the last part of the game when we played these guys in Tucson. The truth is, you guys played like dog poop. No energy, no passion. Nothing, It was embarrassing to me and I hope for you.

"Nothing good ever happens without passion. [by now I am stomping around and jumping up and down] You need to go out and play the game the way God intended it to be played. It's not acceptable to just go through the motions.

"You are way too talented to waste your talents that way... "You need to give a crap, "[my voice was getting louder and louder by this time], "you need to play like you mean it...

"Do you want to be mediocre and play like dog meat, or do you want to show people who you are....

"Passion gentlemen, passion, play like thisis the last game you'll ever play.

"Do you understand me. Do you!"

Suddenly they were on their feet, jumping up and down, filled with the energy missing last time I saw them play. And yes, they played with passion, and absolutely destroyed the other team with a 16-3 mercy rule win. They then went on to win nine of their last ten, and made it to the State tournament, and a successful season.

During the fall, the squad was invited to play up in Phoenix at the Arizona State University field in a small tournament of "invited" teams.

When we got to the field they once again asked for a speech. So I gave them the who wants to be a champion speech.

"Who wants to be a champion?" I asked. All hands were raised.

"Who is willing to do the work necessary to become a champion?

Here's what it takes. You need to start today, this very minute. It isn't enough to talk a good game, it is your job to pay the price it takes to be a champion. You have to start right now doing the right things, not just once in a while, but all the time. You need to hustle all over the field, you need to be good teammates, and you need to pay attention to every detail.

When Johnny Bench (maybe the greatest catcher ever) went for a pop up in the World Series, the ball bounced out of his glove, but right into the glove of Pete Rose. When Rose was asked about it later he simply stated, it was no big deal, because he was 'doing what he was supposed to be doing.'

When the Yankees and Royals were in the world series, on a ball hit to right, Derek Jeter ran from short almost to the first base dugout, caught a poor relay throw and flipped it to home for a monster out. 'No big deal,' he said, 'I was where I was supposed to be.'

One year Arizona was playing Stanford for the PAC championship. A ball was hit deep in the right field corner.

The right fielder relayed the ball to the second baseman who turned and threw a ball way over the head of the Wildcat third baseman and which was surely going to go into the stands.

Instead, the U of A left fielder made an amazing dash from left field and leaped high in the air to keep the ball from going in the stands, caught the ball, and threw it to third for the out.

Arizona then went on to win the National Championship. When asked about the play, and the hustle he said: 'That's where I was supposed to be.'

That's what we need to do. And everyone has to buy in."

They bought in, won the tournament, and played terrific baseball.

Another year I had a really terrific Little League team. We went 23-1-1 and also won our regional regular season team tournament. When we played for the championship we played a team with sixteen home runs to our zero. We had a bunch of little kids who loved to play, and ran bases like wild men.

After practice each day I liked to bring the kids together and review some of the things we learned or worked on that day, some of things we needed to do better and some of the things we would do at our next practice.

We'd bring the kids together to do this, but all they seemed to want to do was play "grab ass" and sass one another (They were twelve year olds, after all). We just couldn't get them to cooperate and focus. They didn't want to listen (after all, they paid attention throughout practice). At first I was a bit aggravated. Then we decided that we had to go at it in a different way.

Instead of talking to them, we let them lead the discussion. Who was the most valuable player in practice today? Who acted like the biggest goof ball? Who paid the most attention? Who behaved the worst? Etc.

Suddenly they were engaged, and this became one of their favorite parts of practice.

Like I said, every team and every player is different. You have to be flexible.

For the most effective pre-game ever, I didn't even utter a word. We were getting ready to play a very good team (the World Champion Legion team from Las Vegas) with a couple of future major leaguers. I could tell our team was very, very nervous.

For once their bravado seemed to leave them. They were actually intimidated. I gathered them together hoping to loosen them up. It didn't work. Nothing seemed to work. I needed to pull a coaching rabbit out of the hat, but I simply didn't have any to pull out. I was desperate.

I knew we would not play very well unless something happened to get them going.

Nothing I could do would loosen them up. Suddenly, one of the players gave off with an unbelievably loud (and smelly) fart. Another giggled, then two more, and then another fart, and all of a sudden they were laughing and farting to beat the band. No words were necessary. They went out and kicked butt.

Chapter 17

Sliding A Lost Art

I have coached hundreds, maybe thousands of kids. Not one that I can remember came to us really knowing how to slide (except for those daredevils who slide head first).

Except for my teams, I have not met a coach throughout the levels of Little League and Club ball that spent any time whatsoever on sliding. I think that's mostly because most of them don't know how to slide themselves. I've seen attempts to teach sliding at various baseball camps. You know, the ones that bring out cardboard and have kids take a couple of slides apiece.

Many coaches use the absence of cardboard as a reason why they don't teach sliding. Truly, that is a sorry excuse. I've taught sliding to thousands, and have never needed to use cardboard as an excuse. When you steal second, there will be no cardboard at the end to greet you.

All of my teams, from t-ball on up work on sliding regularly. I learned to teach sliding the hard way.

One fall, I had a group of really talented 13-14 year olds. Many of them had gone to the Little League World Series, and were USA Champions before getting dismantled by Taiwan. Three of our kids threw 80 or better, and one threw 48.

As usual, we traveled to a tournament (this time in Las Vegas) to play the best Fall teams in America (we were told), with just our ten players.

These were accomplished players. The field was somewhat wet, and I warned the kids about it. In the top of the first, my big first baseman attempted to steal second, and broke his ankle on a very poor attempt at a slide.

From that moment on, I never went to a tournament or played a game unless and until I was sure that our players knew how to slide.

Our technique is really quite simple.

I have all of the kids sit on the ground with their shoes off, legs straight in front of them. I then tell them to jump up, and throw one of their legs under them in a figure four.

The leg that naturally goes underneath becomes their tucked leg for every slide they do from then on out. The last thing we want is someone not to know which leg to tuck. Indecision makes for poor and dangerous sliding.

We have them jump to their tuck at least twenty or thirty times before we attempt any sliding. We then stand, get in a couple of lines, and run toward a coach, sliding on the grass (not cardboard). Arms up off the ground (we don't want them dragging their arms which is nothing but an injury waiting to happen), butt and tucked leg sliding on the grass.

At every practice everyone owes me three good slides. It does take some longer to learn than others. Like anything else, you can't give up, you need to keep doing it. Sooner or later, even the most sluggish will learn.

When sliding is done, they put their shoes on, and we're ready to move forward in practice. We work hard to get everyone to slide hard and quick, and to not slow down before the bag.

When everyone gets the hang of it, we begin to add "popping up" and sliding to various sides of the bases. We work hard at accelerating into our slides, and getting down far enough from the base to help us avoid high tags.

Within a week or two, everyone on the field can "slide." We really emphasize the aspect of actually sliding on the grass, much as like when they are on a slip and slide.

Before every game we alert the umpires to watch the attempted high tags, because we want to get to bases low and quick. Since we began adding sliding to our practices, I've not had another broken ankle. Sore butts, yes. Broken bones, no!

Another thing about sliding, once kids get over their natural fear, they love to do it.

Plus, when they slide, their uniforms get dirty, and they actually look like they've been playing baseball! Sorry, Moms, but a dirty uniform is a badge of honor for a ball player.

Chapter 18

Just When You Think You
Have It All Figured Out, You Don't

When you think you have it all figured out, think again. I learned that lesson last in 2015 when I was a much younger man. It only took me 53 years of coaching to learn this important lesson. Just goes to show, we are never too old to learn. Or perhaps, that makes me really, really stubborn.

In the Spring of 2015 while working out with a grandson and a friend of his, getting ready for Little League try-outs, I was approached by a friend who was looking for a coach for a 50-70 (50 foot pitcher's mound, 70 foot bases) Little League team.

Fifty-70 is basically an attempt by Little League to bring 12 and 13 year olds up a notch, closer to playing real baseball, with leads, and picks and such things, probably an attempt to compete with Club teams that all play "real baseball."

I agreed to coach the team. I prepared and practice as I always do. Many, reps, small groups (pretty easy to do with a roster of ten), competition within practice, catching many fly balls, lots of practice, and plenty of bull pen work for our pitchers.

Lots of line game and one strike game. Pretty good, huh?

After all, I had the winning formula. I could not remember ever having a losing season and knew (or thought I knew) that I would not start with a losing season this year.

Wrong!

Despite hours of repetition on all the tried and true baseball things we'd been doing for years and years, we didn't field, throw, catch, block or pitch (or apparently, coach) very well. Horror of horrors, despite everything I did, we didn't win.

I literally tried everything.

For example, we were horrible in the outfield, so I decided that if we would do nothing but catch fly balls for a week of practice.

500 flies were not enough, we'd do a thousand.

By gosh, I would teach these guys to handle balls in the outfield, or die trying. We worked, and we worked!!!

We had the kids in groups of three, with three coaches hitting fly balls, one after another. They would learn how to play the outfield if it was the last thing we ever did.

Finally game time. We were ready.

The first pitch of the game was what should have been a single to left field. Instead, it went through the legs of our left fielder, all the way to the fence for three bases.

The second pitch was a routine can of corn to our center fielder. Surely it would be caught. Instead, the fielder ran in too far, misjudged the ball into a four base error, over threw the cutoff man (but I'm not sure the cutoff would have caught it, anyway), and here we were, down two after only two pitches.

Some great coach I turned out to be. We continued to work hard the entire season, and only got marginally better.

Once I had that unsuccessful season behind me, I moved on, hoping that I had not totally forgotten how to coach and relate with youngsters.

Even though I was apparently terrible, I was offered a second chance.

A local, and generally successful, high school, after a poor High School season, lost it's head coach to it's biggest rival. That should have tipped me off.

The head of the boosters called me and asked if I would take over and run the school's fall program, or until a new head coach was appointed, a notoriously slow process in the Tucson Unified School District.

The team was full of promise, with at least ten returning seniors from a team that missed out on the State Playoffs the year before.

I showed up the next day for a "field day" and could not help but be pleased by the energy, enthusiasm and excitement surrounding the program, and the money expended by the boosters on field improvements, a fact that should have alerted me to be careful.

Yet I still felt sure this would be a good experience.

The following day, Saturday would be our first practice. Little did I know, that disaster was in the waiting room, waiting for me.

We planned on having about twelve kids come out, but instead had twenty-four.

I spoke to the players about our plans for the Fall, and how I wanted them to work together and play together during the Fall to prepare them as a "team" to challenge for State honors.

State championships are won now, not by waiting until the start of Spring practice I told them.

This was apparently the wrong thing to do, since a number of the prima donna's didn't want to be "stuck" playing for their high school, when they could be playing on ego teams such as a local Yankee Scout team that has never had anyone drafted by the Yankees within my memory.

Exposure, you know. You can't make it to the major leagues without exposure. The heck with your teammates.

I then told them we would be practicing at least three days per week.

Wrong again. They needed time to relax during the Fall. Why practice when they could play on ego teams during the weekend without wasting time on mid week practices.

I then explained that we would be working on fundamental things. I told them I wanted to work on moving our feet in infield, and to work on controlling outfield drops (they had nine the previous season), and wanted to have pitchers throw regularly according to a pattern I outlined for them.

Wrong! wrong! wrong! They didn't need or want to work on fundamentals, that was what Little Leaguers did.

After my little speech (that I learned later was not received well at all), we divided the group. I had four catchers put on their gear with four pitchers in the bull pen. I wanted them to work on location.

Outfielders were divided into groups of three and were to work on drop steps, crow hops, moving to the ball. Infielders were placed in similar groups to work on moving their feet ("one two catch, one two throw") both with and without gloves.

Every player in the program caught dozens of fly balls, dozens of ground balls, and every pitcher got to throw. There was no standing around. Everyone was moving and engaged in one activity or another during the entire practice.

We even had fun playing a 12 on 12 game of one pitch. We concluded with a running game. I was somewhat nervous about what I saw as a lack of hustle, but could work on that on following practices.

I really thought that overall we had a great practice. Especially good for a first practice, getting to know everyone. Everyone seemed energized. Great start, I thought. Wrong again.

I admit that I made a number of mistakes. First of all, I was not Mark, the previous coach (who they didn't particularly like when they had him).

Secondly working on fundamentals was "Little League." Thirdly, I didn't work on situations at all during the first practice. And finally, the biggest mistake of all.

I told the booster head that his kid was more suited for second base than shortstop, and that our catcher needed to completely change his throwing motion.

Nonetheless, stupid as I was, I thought it was a good practice, and a nice way to start the Fall season.

How wrong could anyone be.

That night I received a call from the booster head. I knew it was trouble when I answered the phone. "Mr. Gaynes" the caller said. "This is Mr. Booster."

Since he had always called me by name, I knew it was bad news. He went on: "We have decided to go in a different direction, but thank you for coming out today."

Incredulous I said: "You mean you are firing me after one day!!"

"No, we just decided to move in a different direction."

Even after going down in flames with this group, I was asked to help out with the jv teams at Ironwood Ridge High School in Tucson. Both the Ironwood JV and Varsity played the team that fired me during the High School season.

A great opportunity for revenge.

Our JV had a melt down, and we lost a bunch of our best players, and, as luck would have it, we only had one week to prepare for a road game against the team that canned me.

That would certainly tax our coaching ingenuity. A lot of kids would need to "step up" for us to compete. We juggled our lineup, and practiced hard.

I was nervous as a cat boarding the bus for our 45 minute drive to the other high school. For some reason, this game was very important to me. After all, you don't often get fired after one day coaching at a school!

I told the kids before the game that I would never ask them to win a game for me, but that it would "make me very happy to blow this obnoxious bunch of ninnies off the field."

And so we did. 16-0 mercy rule win. Ah, revenge!

Contrary to my philosophy, (for which I forgave myself on the bus ride home) I actually allowed myself to gloat.

When the booster head came up to me to congratulate us at the end of the game he made a "good game" comment, to which I replied, "I apologize that we didn't field our best team, because we had to dismiss our 6 best players. You see, I can actually coach this game a little."

My wife did not approve. "That's poor sportsmanship" she told me in no uncertain terms.

I agreed with her and could only respond that "the devil made me do it."

I guess I didn't realize how much it hurt my ego to be fired. Still, I was not finished with my pound of flesh.

We got to play that team, again with our varsity during the Arizona State tournament, a game I awaited with great anticipation.

I was on the varsity bench for that game, and got to impart some of what I learned during my day with Sahuaro.

The list of instructions to our team.

1.) The pitcher who was an all region player telegraphed his pitches. We knew whenever a fastball was going to be thrown.
2.) The catcher did not throw well, or accurately, and we could steal second on every first pitch thrown. In fact, to hide the fact that he couldn't even throw back to the pitcher, the catcher would walk halfway to the mound on each pitch and toss the ball to the pitcher.

3.) The shortstop had a rag arm (and should have been at second, just like I told his booster father), and we could semi bunt toward the short stop and be safe all day.

4.) Their best player and an all state quality player (he should have been at short) hit over .500 for the season, but since he played on my Legion team, I knew how to pitch to him. We basically threw off speed stuff away, and fastballs up and purposely out of the strike zone. He was an aggressive but undisciplined hitter.

5.) That team and its prima donnas had no fire, and even had a number of players quit over playing time.

Our head coach thought I was crazy when I told him that we could steal at will off the catcher. It took a couple of runners stealing before he was "all in" with that. Each of my instructions worked, and we bounced them from the playoffs 9-1.

"This is Noah who I got thrown out, and he still likes me. But to this day, he insists he was safe. If you don't believe it, you can ask his friend Aiden."

My revenge was even sweeter when at least six of their players called me after the season asking to play on my Legion team.

It just goes to show that we can't be too smug. Two more examples complete the picture.

In the year 2000 we reached the West Regional Final in Ogden. I had a plan. I saved my ace, Jamie (playing him in left field throughout the tournament) who had pitched a no hitter in Arizona State Legion Championship game.

When Jamie was taken by Boston in the Rule V draft one year, the Red Sox announced that they made that decision after seeing him pitch the State Legion final.

Here he was, rested and ready. Yes, we were perfectly in line to earn a trip to North Carolina for the American Legion World Series. No one could stop us.

Wrong, wrong and wrong again. California came out and scored double digits in runs against Jamie in the first inning and later went on to win the World Series.

Then there was one of the stupidest things ever. Our JV B team was playing in Gilbert, Arizona. We played horribly, but in the last inning we rallied. Runners on first and second, and down one with two of our best hitters up. The hitter singled, and instead of stopping Noah at third, the dumb (very dumb) third base coach (me) sent the runner who represented the tying run. He was thrown out by a mile. Game over!!. We lost.

I still apologize to the team and Noah for that misadventure. Yup, after 55 years of coaching, I sure had it all figured out.

Chapter 19

You Are The Coach, Stand By Your Guns, Remember What Got You There

Many coaches let their parents have too much influence over their preparation, philosophy and teaching. Stick with what you believe in, and what got you there.

One year we played in an experimental nine year old league playing real baseball rules. Leads, stealing, pick offs, balks, etc.

When it was proposed to me that we do so, my reactions was one of shock. "Are you crazy?" I told the head of our local Kino Baseball League. "No nine year old catcher is going to be able to throw out runners. Shoot, they mostly can't even catch the ball when thrown right down the hole!"

"Trust me" he said. "Give it a try." So I did.

It was a real challenge to teach real baseball to nine year olds, most of whom had just finished coach pitch or farm leagues with "dumbed-down" little league rules.

We worked tirelessly at lead-offs, pick offs and steals, and teaching the kids real baseball.

We stole second on every first pitch. Took daring leads. Scored every time possible with scoring leads from second, and worked daily on all of those "real baseball" things.

All of the things I said would happen, happened, yet that was what made that season one of the best ever. Instead of standing around doing nothing, our kids had the time of their lives.

Every kid could steal bases, every kid would get tired and every kid could slide, all of them felt like they were actually playing and contributing. They loved it.

The weakest part of the season was the parents who thought these kids should play like pros, instead of kids learning the game.

One game while stealing second on the first pitch a batter hit a nine year old line drive and our runner was doubled up.

After the game I heard it from a grandparent who told me we had to teach kids to look in, and not get lured into a double play. Others agreed with this person. Yes, I could have changed my philosophy and toned down our base running. Instead, I explained to that person that over the course of the season we would be more successful running, than having the kids go at half speed and look in to find the ball. Most of the parents sided with the grandfather.

I stood my ground. We played our way, the kids had more fun than ever, and not one other runner was doubled off the rest of the season.

We took large leads. Grandpa didn't like that either. A couple of kids were actually picked. Once again I explained that a kid couldn't learn to lead and get back without running the risk of being picked.

"If they were never picked," I explained, "they would never learn how to lead, how to anticipate and how to run bases."

I faced a lot of resistance during the first part of the season.

But because the kids enjoyed it so much, and had such fun, and learned so much, the resistence evaporated, though Grandpa still looks at me with disdain when we come in contact.

That was not the only issue we clashed over.

It is unbelievable no matter where you go, and what level of baseball you watch, there are folks present yelling at players to keep their "elbows up" when they are hitting.

Where the heck did that come from?

Do not keep your elbows up, it will keep you from maximizing your potential as a hitter. There are a number of reasons.

First of all, the bat should be held in your fingers (just as in golf), not your palms, with your door knocking knuckles lined up.

Secondly, hold a bat at your shoulders in your fingers, and try to pick your elbow up. What happens? The bat is no longer in your fingers. Your hands rotate as you raise the elbow. No longer do you have an optimum grip of the bat.

Thirdly, you will now have successfully slowed your bat speed. Once lost, you probably won't ever get it back.

Try swinging a bat from that position. It simply doesn't work. Fourthly, the higher you raise that elbow, the quicker the elbow drops, and with the elbow dropping to your side, the barrel of the bat drops. Say goodbye to line drives. You will, however, give the catchers in your league a lot of practice going after foul pop ups.

Finally, you may never hit an inside pitch again.

Yes, some major leaguers will have their elbows up while in their stance, but after loading and getting ready to hit, their elbows are in a power position.

If you don't believe me, Google "Bad hitting advice" or "keep your back elbow up" and read some articles on the subject.

Stick to your guns, and please, quit with the elbow up business will you.

That does not mean that you should not surround yourself with great coaches. I have sure been lucky in that regard.

The team that beat the mutant was one of those. That team had such wonderful coaches, I couldn't have picked up a greater group. For example, we had fly ball Manny as one of our coaches.

He could literally drop a fungo on a dime. He was so good that during an entire Little League season we amazingly did not have one outfield drop.

We had Roger W and his son (now a nationally known University of Arizona golfer). Roger is a Hall of Fame coach who won State Titles at local Canyon Del Oro High School and took Pima College to the JC World Series. Our other coach was my friend Steve a former college player and a well known Tucson CPA.

And then there was me.

I'll never forget how the Sausage won us a championship.

As I left the field a parent from the other team stomped up to me, confronted me, and let me know under no uncertain circumstances that: "You would be nothing without your coaches!!!!"

I thanked her, and told her that "I guess I'm just not as dumb as I look."

Chapter 20

Patience, Patience, Patience

Baseball is the world's greatest game. It's also the most difficult to teach and play. Virtually every American male has played the game with varying degrees of success, and is therefore an "expert." Unfortunately, most of these "experts" often do more harm than good. When I was a Little Leaguer playing for my Dad we had our league's best pitcher. When he pitched we won. During one July 4th weekend, no games were scheduled. When we got back, we were playing our fiercest rivals. Our ace was on the mound, except that it wasn't our ace.

Over the weekend his uncle, one of those self styled "experts," changed his arm motion. He was suddenly a mediocre pitcher with a poor arm circle. No matter what my Dad did, he could not recapture the magic. All the patience in the world didn't work in that case. Patience comes in many forms. Those who have coached as long as I have are well aware that we need patience to deal with those well meaning experts who know how to play the game, kids with attitude, administrators (often well meaning), rule makers, and, of course, parents. In the long run, repetition and patience are important assets.

Hitting a baseball is still the most difficult thing in sports. Fear of the little white sphere touches everyone who has ever played the game. Kids don't learn to hit, throw or field without guidance. You must be patient. Teach the game the right way. For example, it drives me crazy to watch coaches hit ground balls to infielders who simply sit and wait for the ball, who throw with horrible mechanics and have injury causing arm motions, who believe the appropriate swing is the uppercut, and who fail to keep their front shoulder from turning before contact away from the ball.

To correct these problems takes work, and patience. To institute our philosophy we have had to bite our tongue, more than once.

Chapter 21

Some Of Our Best Games

This book is sprinkled with special games played by our teams, but they are not the only ones. We barely reached the surface. This is a rundown of some of our other truly memorable games.

1.) The Championship Game Of The 64 Team Single Elimination Memorial Day Tournament Run By Canyon Del Oro Little League.

When we drafted our Frontier Little League A's, we had no way of knowing what kind of team we would have. They were small, for sure, wouldn't hit for much power, and didn't have any one dominating little league pitcher. We started out with a decent but not outstanding record of 7-4. We won a couple before we entered the extremely challenging sixty four team CDO tournament.

We knew we were undertaking a great deal. We would have to win 6 in a row against some of the most formidable Little League opposition anywhere during the Memorial Day Weekend.

We played wonderful ball, and won five in a row. One of the teams we beat fired their League's head umpire when he dared tell our pitcher and catcher in a 1-0 victory that this was the best pitched and caught game he had seen all year.

The kids stepped up. Despite having no power ourselves, we reached the finals by beating a team that had hit more than 20 home runs to our none. We won with Rusty on the mound 2-1. All of their players towered over ours.

This, improbably, got us to the championship game against a powerful CDO team with a future Arizona State Quarterback on the mound. To celebrate getting to the "ship," we had an impromptu pizza party at the field from a local chain, MaMa's Pizza, that provided pizza to the park where we were playing.

Fun and merriment was had by all until all of a sudden one of our players vomited up his pizza. That was followed in short order by our other players getting violently ill as well. Each of the kids was wracked by terrible stomach pains. What a time to have your team come down with food poisoning.

In addition to treating the kids (and some parents as well), we had to figure out how we could play the championship game. Some of the players could not get out of bed the next day.

Others could not get through warmups without excusing themselves to run to the bathroom. Somehow we needed to get it together to play a game. The kids would absolutely not settle for a forfeit when we had come so far.

We ran a shuttle to the bathroom all game long. We sent those who would not hit for a while or were down in the order to the bathroom so they could hopefully be ready to hit when their time came.

Believe me, they left a trail of vomit alongside the dugout. Disgusting, yes, but that did not stop our kids. They had a baseball game to play. They willed themselves to play.

"1987 Frontier Little League A's Pizza Eating Team."

Yes, they won that game, and did not lose again that season. We ended the year, 30-4.

They were tournament champions.

After the game there was a trophy celebration and a number of other awards. The MC then made an announcement:

"Congratulations to the Frontier A's who, in addition to their trophies have won a pizza party at MaMa's Pizza."

2.) KFC Vs. World Connie Mack Champion Arizona Firebirds

As has happened again and again throughout the years, the High Desert Classic in Albuquerque, which assembled some of the best teams in America year after year, resulted in some of the most terrific games involving some of the most terrific teams in America.

One year, KFC ended up head to head against America's best team, the Arizona Firebirds, winners that year of the Connie

Mack World Series. KFC's 10 players were simply no match for the 18 or more talented Firebirds.

The Firebirds had more arms than KFC had players. As usual, when the Firebirds played, there were sure to be a legion of pro scouts in attendance.

Physically, the Firebird players dwarfed our group. They had arms, power, and played terrific defense. They were certainly a formidable group. One of the most formidable I had ever seen in my many years of coaching.

They were one of those teams that looked imposing, just getting off the bus. Our players were intimidated just being around them at the hotel pool.

They had absolutely pounded every singe team they played. They actually had more home runs in the thin Albuquerque air than we had hits. We had no chance against those guys.

As expected, we fell behind early. We scratched out a run here and there, but were down three in the last inning.

As usual, we didn't give up, tied the score and actually had the potential winning run on third.

In the eighth inning they scored to go up one. We fought back and tied the game. In the ninth, they scored again, and left the bases loaded, and once again we tied the game. The same pattern repeated in the 10th, except they scored two off our exhausted pitcher, Chad, who though tired, refused to come out of the game. We once again tied it against their flame throwing closer.

In the eleventh with two down a Firebird lofted a high fly to right field. We thought for sure the inning would be over. Instead, our right fielder dropped the ball and let in what became the winning run.

After over three hours of tense baseball, against the best team in the country, we ran out of magic. Game over. But, we were proud of our kids.

3.) Tucson July 4 Championship Game vs. Bryce Harper And His Las Vegas Teammates

For years, I would organize a Tucson, July 4 weekend tournament. We've been fortunate to have a spate of good teams from New Mexico, Louisiana, Nevada, and California in attendance. Always good competition.

One year we had a very powerful group in from Las Vegas, complete with Bryce Harper. As usual, the Las Vegas team was big and deep with a plethora of arms.

We had Joey and Kyle, our aces, ready on the mound.

The game was taut all the way. It was tied after 7 and went into extra innings and stayed that way until the tenth.

The Vegas third baseman was a young man named Campbell. He was perhaps the biggest man I have ever seen. Everything about him was huge. He stood at least 6'7" with huge muscular arms, hands and legs. He was just big, not fat.

In the top of the tenth with the potential winning run on base he hit a towering fly ball to center field. The field was large, major league dimensions.

The field was used by the Rockies for Spring Training. It was obvious that his ball would go out of the park.

At the crack of the bat, Jacob, our centerfielder turned his back to home plate ala Willie Mays against the Indians in the 1954 World Series. Full speed he ran to the wall, and at the last second, up against the fence, he jumped and made one of the greatest catches ever.

Campbell was almost to second when the ball was caught. And after it was caught, he hightailed it on a line to our center fielder. "Oh, no!!" we thought. "He's going to kill Jacob." He didn't slow as he ran toward Jacob. "Poor Jacob"

I moaned, helpless to stop the massacre about to happen. As Campbell got to Jacob, he yelled to him "that was the hardest ball I ever hit and the best catch I've ever seen."

He hugged Jacob, and picked him up. The danger was over, Jacob was safe. To this day that was one of the most marvelous acts of sportsmanship I'd ever seen. Three outs, we were still in the game.

In the bottom of the tenth, our catcher, Ray, who was in a disastrous slump and missed a couple of games got a base hit to win the game.

4.) Semifinal Game Of The High Desert Classic Against American Legion World Champion Bishop Gorman From Las Vegas

We have had a number of epic duels against always loaded Bishop Gorman. As always, they were loaded with future major leaguers.

As always, we had our ten men of iron. Seemingly, we were underdogs with little chance to win. As always, we were down to our last pitchers. We pitched a youngster who played junior college ball in Oregon. I had never seen him pitch but had faith that he could do the job. And what a job he did. He held them down, inning after inning.

One of the better played games. Each team made every play, and each pitcher got the big outs when they were needed.

Once again we were deadlocked in extra innings. Try as they might, neither team could break through. Another game between us that was fit for champions. No one wanted to lose, and tempers were near the surface. The Gorman coaches were as tense as we were.

In the bottom of the ninth our shortstop, Sebastian, got a hold of one and sent everyone home. In fact, that's just what he did. As he rounded the bases he not so graciously wished our Las Vegas counter parts "nice rides home."

Well, it took me quite some time to calm the Las Vegas team and their coaches down.

These were big folks. We really didn't want to mess with them. The only people bigger than the Gorman players were their coaches. I finally helped calm everyone down and evinced an apology from Sebastian. That was a difficult way to end a terrific baseball game.

5.) KFC Vs. Tucson High For The Arizona State Championship

I received a call one day from a former player who was coaching a high school team in the Tucson area.

He told me he had a pitcher who he wanted to get some experience at a higher level of play. Ryan came to us with one of the funkiest wind ups ever. Not only that, he had one of the best change ups ever. I asked him to change his style of pitching to use his change up as an out pitch.

Once he did that, he became one of the most formidable pitchers in the state of Arizona.

He exploded on the scene by immediately becoming the nemesis of our arch rival, Tucson High. If they didn't get to him early in the count, he'd have them flailing away at his change up. He shut them out in his first game. He beat them at least 10 times on his way to becoming the all time KFC leader in wins. No matter what approach they took against him, Ryan prevailed.

Up came the State Legion Tournament. As usual it was Tucson (Post 7) and KFC in the hunt for the State Championship.

This time they were loaded for bear. It seemed like Ryan's magic was gone as they rang up a five spot in the first inning.

One of the Post 7 Dads, the father of a former major leaguer, was particularly obnoxious, and made all kinds of insulting remarks about Ryan, and his "hitability."

He exhorted their players to "get on the merry go round." All of Tucson's frustration about facing Ryan had boiled to the surface, as they racked up hit after hit against Ryan. Yes, it looked very dark for us.

This was particularly apparent when their pitcher was obviously on his game. As usual, we fought from behind, and finally tied the game in the 9th, and then went up one.

With one out and runners on second and third, a Tucson hitter hit what would clearly be the game winner, a fly ball to right.

Brandon, our right fielder took off, it seemed clear that the ball would hit the ground fair and end our latest run at a state championship, when Brandon took off on a dive, somehow coming up with the ball in mid air, firing a strike to home from the ground, doubling off the runner from third who, perhaps taking for granted that he would score at least the tying run, lollygagged on his way home and was beaten by the ball.

Out number three. Game over. We were state champs one more time.

6.) West Regionals, KFC Vs. Bishop Gorman

Bishop Gorman brought an all star aggregation to the West Regional tournament in northern California. Both teams were loaded. Gorman had at least 5 future major leaguers, and KFC had a couple themselves. There were at least 9 future D-1 players on the field. The talent level was amazing.

Of course, KFC played from behind. We were pitching Cody, a crafty lefty who didn't seem to fool Gorman any. In the first inning our catcher threw out a runner trying to steal third. The ball beat the runner substantially. Safe yelled the umpire. "What!"

In the second inning the same thing happened, and once more Ray threw him out. Safe the umpire yelled again. I couldn't hold it in any more, and went out and confronted the umpire. I had seen this umpire all week, and knew, just knew, he would be bad for us. And bad he was!

Well, I got the old heave ho.

Nonetheless, we continued to fight back. In the bottom of the ninth with two outs and the bases loaded, we were down three with Ray our catcher up. He hit a long towering fly to right. Clearly it would be over the fence. Joey Gallo, now a major league star, who seemed to be at least 7' tall, backed up against the fence, jumped, and caught a sure home run.

Game over. We gave it everything, but fell short in one of the most exciting games ever.

7.) Our Senior League A's Vs. San Xavier Senior Little League

One of our biggest little league rivalries through the years Rusty played Little League with us was against the teams from the San Xavier Little League

We had amazing games, starting with the time "Big Jim" (who in later years wasn't so big as others caught up to him)) burst on the scene and beat us for the Tucson Toros Youth Winter Baseball League minors championship.

The San Xavier League was primarily Native American. Boy, did those folks love their baseball! The games at their beautiful field were always packed with their extended families and friends.

Of the games, the Senior League semifinals at their park, was one of the most memorable games ever.

As usual the park was full (many more of their fans than ours), with a large festive group hanging out adjacent to our dugout. When a San Xavier player hit a grand slam in the first inning, the fans were alive.

We had won the last few games between our leagues, and they were sure they would win this one! The onslaught continued into the second inning. By the time we took a breath, we were down 9-0. The San Xavier fans were howling.

We did everything we could, changing pitchers at will. By the fourth, the tide had slowed. We even put a couple of runs on the board. By the sixth we were down one. We tied it in the 6th when the lights went out. Curfew.

We came back the next day, and suddenly a pitcher's duel broke out. The score stayed tied in the 7th, 8th, 9th, and 10th. In the 10th we finally got some runners on, and threatened to score.

With two out, we had runners on first and second with Rusty, a switch hitter, hitting lefty, at bat. I was coaching third. My instructions to my runner at second were to take the longest lead he possibly could to try and draw a throw or two, even if he would be in danger of being picked off. Our goal was to get the shortstop to play closer and closer to second.

When the shortstop at the urging of his coach moved over, Rusty hit a hard ground ball right through the spot vacated by the shortstop. Our runner (who later ran the soccer team FC Tucson) took off with contact, and beat the throw home. We had won a tense and draining game.

As we packed up to leave, the group of festive folks who were camped by our dugout came toward me as a group. "Hey, Coach" they yelled as they approached. They had been loud all night, and I'm sure there was plenty of alcohol. To say I was intimidated would be a real understatement. As they continued to gain on me, yelling to me, I knew I was in deep, deep trouble. "Hey, Coach, Hey Coach!"

When they got close, they grabbed me, but instead of what I feared, they started patting me on the back and complimenting me. "Coach, you're smart, we saw what you did, making our shortstop cover so your kid could hit in the winning run."

They looked over at the San Xavier coach, "him, not so much." They didn't want me to leave, but instead wanted to talk about the game. These people knew and loved baseball. They were great fans.

Soon our folks joined us for quite the post game celebration.

8.) KFC Vs. Post 52, Area A. Semifinals

For years, one of KFC's traditional rivals was Post 52 from Sierra Vista coached by John Sands, Terry Francona's backup during Arizona's National Championship run. John is quite the character, and would get his team's attention emulating a train whistle. He's now umpiring full time (don't let him know I admitted this, but he is really a pretty good umpire).

Generally his teams were loaded. This particular year they were blessed with three or four really good pitchers, and a couple of sluggers. He had two 90 mph pitchers ready to go.

One of them, Carl became a D-1 player and now coaches the Junior Varsity at Buena High School in Sierra Vista, AZ. The other, Donnie, was a big lefty and future major leaguer. We had our hands full.

As usual, we were short of pitching. As a result we decided on throwing our 6'8" center fielder. Brad had only thrown a couple of innings for us all year, but he came ready to play.

Aside from a monster home run by Tyler, the Post 52 behemoth, the pitchers of both teams threw inning after inning of blanks. We scratched out a couple of runs to tie the game at 2 after regulation.

It seemed that each team threatened every inning, and defensively, the teams made play after play. The game was a classic, and up for grabs as we entered the 10th inning.

In the 10th we scratched out a run to go up 3-2. In the bottom of the inning Post 52 got runners on first and second. With one out, the hitter smashed what, to this very day John, who was coaching third, claimed was a walk off fair ball. He swears that(and he will go to his grave believing that) the ball hit chalk and the game should have been over.

After we got the second out, Tyler was up. John remembers our outfielders playing practically at the fence (the field was very large at the University of Arizona). Tyler took a number of healthy hacks, before striking out and ending one of the great games ever.

9.) KFC Vs. Tucson High, Semifinals Of The Arizona State Legion Championships

As usual, rivals KFC and Tucson High were the top competitors in the American Legion State Championships, this particular year held in Phoenix, Arizona.

As usual the game was nip and tuck, nip and tuck. Neither team could get much of a lead, and when they did, they couldn't hold on to it. Back and forth it went, and as usual, the game was tied after 9, and went, into extra innings.

Tucson went ahead in the 11th. We got a couple of men on when Michael, our all American second baseman came up to bat.

Our hopes were on Mike who played more games for us than anyone in our history. He was a regular for us starting as a thirteen year old, after he had played his last Little League game. He volunteered to travel the 90 miles to Sierra Vista to play for us against always powerful Post 52, a team that was particularly dangerous at home.

As luck would have it, Mike was facing Arizona's 3A pitcher of the year. The very first pitch came right toward Mike's ear hole.

As he dove for the ground, I could see panic written all over his face.

He had never seen a ball thrown so hard, and especially one spinning for his head. He got up off the ground shaken, and the look he threw me was a devastating one. I called time to give him some time to recuperate. When Mike was ready, and as he took the box, you could see that the pitcher was ready for him. Nothing off speed to this kid.

Mike told me that he knew he would get another fastball, so he dug in, and got ready. Sure enough, a fastball was coming his way. This one was right down the middle, and Mike swung, hit it right back at the pitcher (who was forced to duck) and through the middle to centerfield for a base hit.

From that point on, I knew Mike was special. Had he not had a catastrophic injury, he would have been a major leaguer.

In the bottom of the 11th, with two out Mike marched to the plate. Could Mike make his magic as he had so often done in the past?

Though quite thin, Mike had the ability to loft the ball. Our hopes were pinned on Mike. As usual, Mike delivered. A three run walk off home run. We had beaten the mighty Badgers.

10.) The Greatest Little League Game Ever Played

My grandson Mathias played with us some years after Rusty did. Though not blood relatives, their games had a lot in common. Both hit best in the clutch, both were terrific age group pitchers who didn't throw very hard, and both played the best against the better competition. Because I had good feelings about the team Mathias played on, and in memory of our great A's team that Rusty played on, we named them the A's as well. We hoped to capture lightening in a bottle. They were the team that dominated the "mutant" that was mentioned earlier. They seemed to embody the attributes of a team that we all idealized.

My friend and co-coach Steve Phillips explains the background for the game he calls "the greatest Little League game ever played."

"If you cannot beat them…join them," said Steve in an all too familiar quote that I lived with almost on a weekly basis in the summer of 2006.

Because you see that was the Little League summer that I coached my son against another Little League team coached by some old guy whose name I did not even know.

What I did know, was that no matter what I did, no matter how good I thought my players were prepared, he would win. Nothing ever fancy, or out of the norm, just simple things that his team always seemed to do better than mine…..run bases, throw strikes and catch fly balls.

So getting back to the quote at the beginning of this paragraph, I got tired of losing to this old guy always holding a score book while he coached third base (in his sandals), so I employed a new tactic….I would meet this guy and see if we could coach together.

"That fall I humbled myself with the realization that I would probably never beat this coach and I introduced myself to Coach Alex Gaynes. Little did I know that introduction would lead to my experiencing several of the most amazing baseball teams and seasons in my life.

The first team that I had the honor of coaching with Alex was our nine year old fall team (league age ten), the Indians. After losing our first five games, and a few minor roster and coaching adjustments, our small (in both numbers and stature) team went on to win the next fourteen games in a row including the league championship game.

I remember distinctly Coach Alex telling me 'enjoy this, it doesn't happen very often'. Coach, I am so delighted to say how wrong you were. We later experienced an amazing twelve year old Little League season, which included facing an alien player and an amazing league championship tournament with the deck stacked against us. From that point starting with our "miracle" Cruisers team, made up of players from a local parochial school, and then to winning three consecutive state championships with your help in securing the Hanson coaching team at Desert Christian High School, we were baseball blessed.

"But one of my fondest memories was the "greatest little league game ever played." A game that spanned three days, four come from behind must score situations, no pitching left, a tournament schedule stacked against us, and once again facing a team that was overall more talented, bigger, stronger and faster than our guys.

"But this game was truly the mountaintop example of players believing in themselves and their teammates, never giving up, and never believing that they were finished in a game until the final out.

"A game that included every single player contributing a do or die moment, parents and fans thinking the game was over and we had lost multiple times, yet when the chips were down, sometimes by multiple runs in the bottom of an inning, yet still finding a way to tie the game and send it into yet another inning, and twice into another day.

"The final inning will forever remind me that the game is never truly over until it is over. . .as a coach I never want to think that the game is lost until that moment, but that last inning I truly had my doubts. Down by two, with the bottom of the lineup coming up…and in less than five minutes we would walk away the victors. Two outs, bases empty, a hit, a walk, a hit batter, still zero runs in our bottom half of the inning, and thirty seconds later the game would be over in our favor. A past ball and a wild throw back to the catcher, and 72 hours of baseball had finally come to an end with the W next to our team."

It was truly a coaching carousel that we were lucky to be on Appreciate the good times, they end way to soon.

After Mathias quit baseball, Alex and I were watching a game together. I'm afraid I was a little harsh when my son, who was actually a very good ball player, struck out.

Alex came up to me and whispered to me: "Steve, I only wish I could watch Mathias strike out one more time."

As a digression, I though it would be fun to note that Steve who wrote the blurb about the "greatest game" was also part of a fun story.

I noted previously that I coached a Sun Belt College League team for a number of years. For Steve's 45 birthday I thought it would be neat if he got to play a game with his son, Ryan. Though I probably violated league rules, I started Steve at second base. I realized that it was a little unfair to play him in that game because we were facing a D-1 lefty submariner with really mean "stuff." He was so good, he struck out my D-1 drafted shortstop three times in a row. The rest of the team flailed away in frustration as well.

I was supposed to be Steve's friend, and here I was, putting him in the Lion's den. Steve had been a decent player, and even played junior college baseball. But that was more than 20 years earlier. But win or lose, he would fulfil a Dad's dream to play side by side with his son.

I was coaching third when Steve came to bat. I immediately realized how cruel it was to put him in this spot. I was supposed to be his friend! From the first pitch, I knew he had no chance.

There was a good two feet between his bat and the ball on the first pitch. Strike one! Remember Casey at the Bat? I sure did. It got even worse with pitch number 2.

Steve stepped out of the box, and threw me a look which said, "what have you gotten me into?" He had his own rooting section made up of his wife, friends and family. And here he was, disgracing himself. Steve was nothing if not a proud person.

Reluctantly he knocked some dirt off his cleats and stepped back into the box. The lefty was pretty confident as he got ready to strike Steve out. He went through his corkscrew motion and unleashed another pitch that could not be hit. Steve took a huge breath, got his foot down early, as we instruct our players, took a mighty rip and fouled it off, barely. He would get one more chance.

He got back in the box, looked for and got a fastball, and yes, he hit the ball. I watched, stunned, as the ball cleared the infield and continued to rise until it cleared the left field fence. The fans (me included) and our team went crazy.

Steve did it.

Within hours it seemed like the whole Tucson community had heard the news. A new legend was born.

Chapter 22

American Legion Baseball Has A Special Place In My Heart

I've coached an American Legion Baseball team sponsored by KFC on and off (mostly on) from 1992 to the summer of 2015.

With club teams, high school teams, academy teams and pay for play teams proliferating, people often ask why we stayed with Legion all those years, with its suffocating rules that make it very difficult to compete against Club teams, Academy teams, and Connie Mack teams. We never let that stop us. For the better part of 25 years we competed with the best amateur baseball had to offer.

Legion has a terrific history spanning 94 years. Irascible, and cantankerous Bud Grainger, the long time Area A Commissioner was a part of American Legion baseball from 1941 until his death a few short years ago. He played Legion ball, he coached Legion ball, and he ran Tucson's area A.

Most major leaguers played Legion ball.

Legion is still a team game which embodies the best qualities of the American spirit. On the other hand, Club ball and the select team aggregations, pay for play "academies" and the like resemble AAU basketball more than they do baseball "teams."

Traveling around playing tournaments, and show cases results, not in a team game, but individualists sharing the same field. There is no common goal. It's all for their own "exposure." Our KFC Legion groups are more like family.

We were always different. Few Legion teams traveled the country as we did taking on all comers. We had a motto that we would play anyone, anywhere at anytime, regardless of how formidable they were, how many sets of uniforms they had, or how many D-1 players they advertised.

Legion has strict rules about recruiting players, and has true teams, not city or State wide all star teams. Yes, it made it harder to compete, but we were always ornery enough to welcome it.

As I noted at the beginning, I am a dinosaur, a maverick. There aren't many of us left. My friend Roy is about the only other one left in Tucson. The experiences with our players just don't seem to be matched these days.

Legion was a good part of the difference between us and others.

Legion gave us many unexpected good times and monster experiences.

For example, one year after we won our State Legion Tournament we were scheduled to play in the West Regional Championships in Greeley, Colorado.

Legion flew us out to Denver, at its expense, provided beautiful hotel accommodations, and gave the kids meal money besides. Our kids were treated like major leaguers. I haven't had a player attend Regionals (we've been to 10 of them) that didn't make enough memories for a lifetime.

Legion assigned us local families to act as guides for the week.

Before we left on the plane to Denver, I received a call from our hosts to be. I don't know why, but I answered the phone: "Big Al, here." The caller laughed, and from that time we became friends, and our players were treated like family.

After being picked up from the airport, we were supposed to drive into Greeley for an introductory tournament meeting at the tournament hotel. Instead, we stopped off with our hosts and had a two hour lunch at a Mexican restaurant on the way.

The lunch was provided by our hosts. You would have thought we had all been friends forever.

Well, much to the consternation of tournament officials, we arrived two hours late for our meeting. As a punishment we were informed that we would not be allotted any practice time or bp at the Greeley field.

"Don't worry," our hosts told us. "We will take care of you." They surely did!

We all hopped in our Legion provided vans and followed our hosts and their families to the outskirts of Greeley. It seemed like we drove for miles and miles when we pulled on to a farm road.

As we did so, we could see a farmer in the distance on his tractor. When we approached the tractor, we saw, there, in the middle of nowhere, one of the most beautiful baseball fields in America. I had never seen a nicer one.

We were stunned. We weren't easily stunned. Don't forget, we had been to the Field of Dreams, and also to one of the great fields in America in Fairfield, California.

The field had perfect sod (the owner ran a sod farm), an unbelievably great infield ("better than Coors Field," our hosts told us), and our own personal groundskeeper.

He built this field, so his son would have a place to play when the town field was not available. We had a great time with our hosts, and taking batting practice. We were then invited back to hit the next day, since we didn't play our first game until later in the evening.

When we arrived back at the field the next day we were greeted by our hosts, and a fantastic picnic barbeque lunch. Once again our players were amazed at the hospitality as we all sat down for a terrific lunch. Our boys had immediate friends, and you would have thought the kids that were with us were related to them. "Coach," they asked, "Why are these people so nice to us?"

"It's because they are nice!"

When we played our games, we had our own rooting section. Our hosts, their kids, their friends and our kids visited both before and after our games. We also continued our batting practice and picnic routine.

How wonderful were these folks?

After a batting practice session the owner of the field came over to us with apologies. Whatever, (after all he had done for us) could he possibly have to apologize for? Sadly he shook his head and announced: "I'm sorry, fellas, the field is not available tomorrow."

We later found out why. We shouldn't have been surprised. Greeley is a rural, farm area with hundreds (probably more) of itinerant farm workers employed in the area. On Sundays a barbecue, the ball field and the adjacent soccer field were made available to the workers and their families.

This was a once in a lifetime experience. These were truly "good" people. It made you feel good just being around them.

When we were eliminated from the tournament at least fifty folks gathered together on the field for a massive cry, and good bye hug.

It was simply amazing to watch our 6'8" center fielder hugging a host's ten year old daughter. Our players had tears in their eyes as they said their good byes.

This was one of those experiences that made Legion so extraordinary.

Chapter 23

Coach As Motivator

Like it or not, with all due apologies to Lute Olsen who decried that view, I believe the coach has the job of teaching the kids baseball, and motivating them to be the best they can be.

My approach is to discuss real life examples to motivate them to succeed. Different approaches work with different teams. Some will naturally be more motivated then others. We have found that playing competitive games like our one strike game and our line game are great motivators. Some times the intensity during these games far exceeds the intensity of a real ball game. Some of that intensity rubs off on the parents as well.

We try and get the kids to play in practice as we want them to play in our games. Interestingly, most folks complain about the intensity of their players during practice. We sometimes have the opposite problem, trying to get the players to play as hard in games as they do in practice.

Some players don't want to hear my stories. Other teams beg to have "an inspirational story" or speech before every game. Some teams actually need to be calmed down before they play. It is up to the coach to read their moods, and deal with their ups and downs.

Then there is the issue of motivating individual players rather than the team as a whole. For example, Mychal (who was quoted above) from our 13 year old team was motivated in a very personal way. Motivation is different for every player. The coach needs to be sensitive to each individual player's needs. Even then, you may never know.

I began helping out with the junior varsity program at Ironwood Ridge High School, a Tucson area suburban high school a couple of years ago. I came on board rather late since the approval process for coaches in Tucson has become quite cumbersome.

I wasn't with the program very long when we were set to travel and play in Nogales, Arizona. Year in and year out Nogales fields great baseball teams, and won the State title two years running with the personnel we were playing against that day.

We started a very talented pitcher (he was the best hitter, best pitcher and fastest runner on the team). He was on that day. They could do nothing against him. After beating Nogales, it was clear that he would not be playing many games for us. The varsity was in his immediate future. And sure enough, he did not play any other games for us that season as he became a mainstay both on the mound and in the field for the varsity. Tragically, he did not make it through the season. Somewhere along the line he hurt his arm, and ended up needing Tommy John surgery that kept him off the field for one full high school season, and off the mound for two seasons. When he came back, I was still with the JV, and we had little contact other than to great each other.

Routinely at the end of the jv season (which ends prior to the Varsity season), I help out at the varsity level, mostly telling stories at their request.

IR has a strong program and a terrific Coach, and makes the state playoffs just about every year. I can't remember when they didn't make it. This season, unfortunately we lost our first game and were eliminated. Seth, because of his surgery never got to pitch, though he was a starter on defense.

After our loss, and elimination the coaches were left with the unenviable duty of congratulating the players on a great season, while also acknowledging that we did not go as far as we hoped. Each Coach had his say, and then I was invited to add my two cents. I started out by congratulating the Varsity and its 9 seniors (all starters) for setting a high bar and continuing the tradition of making State every single year.

Then I turned to our lower class men and noted, you don't win a championship in February at the start of the high school season, but you win starting tomorrow. If you want to keep the tradition going you need to start now, especially since we were losing so much talent. I continued along that refrain throwing in comments and stories as well.

When completed, the players and coaches embraced with tears in their eyes. One thing you learn quickly in coaching or playing, the end comes way too soon. Players and coaches need to appreciate every day together. The time is so fleeting.

A Senior at Ironwood Ridge is required to write a major paper concerning what they have learned during their high school careers, how they matured, and those who were most influential and had the greatest impact on them.

When Seth and I hugged, he told me that in his Senior paper he wrote about me as the greatest motivator he knew. I was totally blind sided. I never expected anything like that, and I think that is the sincerest and most wonderful compliment I have ever received. I will always cherish those words. I have trouble telling the story without tearing up.

Coaches have a far greater impact on their players than they ever realize. If I have anything to say, it is for coaches to remember this always in dealing with their players. Yes, as I said before, coaching is really almost a sacred trust. Don't betray it.

Chapter 24

Those You Meet Along The Way

Probably the most difficult part of putting this book together was trying to figure out who, and what to include. The experiences along the way, and those people I have met, have truly made me a rich man in the ways that matter most.

I have met some of the most wonderful folks on my path. Coaches (both who coached with me and against me), players, parents, opponents, friends, acquaintances, and my wonderful extended family (and especially my forgiving, patient wife), certainly have made me feel just like Lou Gehrig when he made his "luckiest man on the face of the earth" speech at Yankee Stadium.

Imagine being 72 years old, never a great athlete, and Coach Kevin has given me the chance to throw hundreds of batting practice pitches a day (in hundred degree weather). And I'm loving every minute of it!

All I can do as I leave the field, is look up at the sky, and thank the Good Lord for his blessings and experiences.

I hope others can share these moments.

I would like to acknowledge all the help and assistance given to me by my editorial board made up of my wife, Pat, and my sister Debbie, and the monumental efforts of my good friend, Lou Pavlovich.